His kiss had left her weak

"Laura." Blaise's voice sounded urgent.

"I'm all right—just leave me alone." She closed her eyes.

"You're a baby." Now he was mocking her. But then he took her hands and held them tenderly. "Come on, you know I'm not capable of that sort of thing."

"Well, that's good. At least you won't try kissing me again," Laura said shyly. "I just felt weak for a moment. It was as if I let you own me."

His dark voice had an edge of amusement. "Open your eyes."

"As you wish." Laura's gray eyes were enormous. "You had no right to kiss me," she added indignantly.

"I want you as much as you want me. In fact, if you weren't a little virgin, I'd have you tonight."

Hunter's Moon

Margaret Way

Harlequin Books

TORONTO • NEW YORK • LOS ANGELES • LONDON
AMSTERDAM • PARIS • SYDNEY • HAMBURG
STOCKHOLM • ATHENS • TOKYO • MILAN

Original hardcover edition published in 1982
by Mills & Boon Limited

ISBN 0-373-02556-4

Harlequin Romance first edition June 1983

CHAPTER ONE

THE big, book-lined office was beginning to grow dim, but still Howard Mitchell, solicitor, whose office it was, made no move to switch on a light. He, like the girl opposite him, sat in a state of near-bemusement. A kindly, astute man, with a wide knowledge of human nature, Howard Mitchell was disturbed and unhappy hurting this young girl he had looked on as someone special since the moment he had met her at the entrancing age of five. Then, she had looked up at him with radiant eyes and held out a small hand like those exquisite little Princesses he had once seen in London, Elizabeth and Margaret Rose. Her father, David Mallory, had brought her in to show her off, proud and delighting in his beautiful little daughter, talking about how smart she was, how adorable, while Howard had stood there smiling and congratulating him. Fifteen years before, and since then many upsets and tragedies.

Now Howard sat forward, shaking his head with deep regret. 'I'm so sorry, Laura. So *terribly* sorry.'

Laura said nothing, but sat quietly, narrow shoulders squared.

'Your father loved you dearly, my dear. You know that.'

Laura dipped her head protectively so the smooth blonde mass of her heavy pageboy fell forward to shield her left cheek. 'Yes,' she murmured sadly, 'it's just that he loved my stepmother and Jamie more.'

Put into words it upset the elderly man desperately.

'It was your father's ambition, of course—a son. He was that kind of man.' Nevertheless, Howard Mitchell, who had heard and seen just about everything when it came to wills, was astonished and seriously disturbed by his late client's actions. Actions unknown to him. Howard's partner, Tom Parker, had called it a 'rotten shame' and suggested what Howard suggested now.

'We can, of course, contest the will,' he said vigorously. 'We have every chance of getting a favourable judgment.'

'I don't want that, Uncle Howard,' Laura answered, her voice low but emphatic.

'Think about it, my dear,' he urged her. 'You've lived a very secure, comfortable life. You're barely twenty years of age, only halfway through your studies, and as it is, you'll be unable to continue full-time. As a matter of fact. . . .'

'But what am I anyway?' Laura suddenly exclaimed, 'a lily of the field who can't toil? I can get a job. I've been far luckier than most. Most people would think it was high time I earned my own living. I've always worked through vacations.'

'But that was different, my dear, just odd jobs. You're not actually qualified for what you want. I've discussed this with Helen and we consider you should continue your studies until you've got your degree. Of course we shall pay for you now and I'm quite certain you'll be able to pay us back later on.'

For an instant Laura's grey eyes swam with tears and she didn't look twenty at all but still five. 'Bless you, Uncle Howard,' she said softly. 'Bless you both.'

'As you have blessed us with your friendship. It isn't every young girl who delights in old fogeys.'

'Then they don't know what pleasure they're missing, how much they can learn.' Laura looked back at him with true affection in her eyes. 'You don't even want paying back, do you? You're just trying to spare my feelings, my pride.'

Howard Mitchell knew full well there was steel in that straight, slender girl's body. 'Helen and I want this for you, my dear,' he said simply. 'Our little friend. The granddaughter we didn't have, if you like.'

'I'll get my degree, certainly,' she said purposefully, 'but it will take a bit longer, that's all. It's high time I stood on my own two feet. They're good feet, I'm pleased to say. And strong, thanks to all that ballet. I'll find a job and continue my studies at night. It's all settled. Paula has the house and the money, she always wanted that, and anyway, I love Jamie, that's why I won't fight anything. In time, it will all come to him. Even if Paula remarries at least Jamie's interests have been well protected. We must be grateful for that.'

A lot of people wouldn't be, Howard considered. The scenes he had witnessed! He continued to look at the girl with undisguised admiration. 'No one could be sweeter to that boy than you are,' he said almost sternly, 'and he adores you, though it doesn't please his mother. I'm sure if Jamie were only older he would insist you have your just share. In my judgment. . . .'

'Which I value most highly.'

Howard Mitchell jabbed aimlessly at a file. 'We must contest the will. You're your father's daughter—his only daughter. He was a rich man, and you're morally entitled to part of his estate.'

'You can't upset yourself,' Laura said warningly, noting the pink spots on the elderly cheekbones. 'You may not think so now, Uncle Howard, but I know I'm blessed. I have my youth and my health and my intelligence. What more could I want?'

'I don't think you understood me, my dear. It's only

fair. It bothers me dreadfully that things have turned out this way. Paula can't leave it like this—she just can't!'

'She can and she will,' Laura answered, not without black humour. 'Besides, Uncle Howard, it was my father's money to leave as he liked. Which he *did*. I won't change anything. I won't try to outwit Paula, and I'll survive.'

'Think on it,' Howard Mitchell said grimly. 'It's not easy fending for oneself, and I've always considered young girls need the protection of their own home.'

'I can flat with some of my friends. I'm *going* to.'

Still the elderly solicitor sat hunched. 'You know your father's reasons, of course, don't you?' He had to reassure the girl at once. 'He simply thought his beautiful daughter would marry early and marry well. After all, you must admit you have any number of admirers, and your father's heart attack was so desperately premature. A man in his prime!' Death came so close at these times. Howard Mitchell picked up the file blindly. 'He thought he would have all the time in the world—to see you happily married, to see his beloved little son grow up. But he died.'

'Yes,' Laura whispered, her shining head bent to one side. It had never bothered her that her father had loved Jamie best. After all, she adored him herself and she would have to learn to live without him. Paula would see to that.

'I'm going to speak to your stepmother,' Howard said forcefully.

'Oh, please don't!' Laura implored.

'Strange woman!' the solicitor mumbled. A strange, hard woman, but beautiful. David Mallory would always marry a beautiful woman, but if only he had married a kind one. Right from the beginning Paula

Mallory had taken no pleasure in her stepdaughter. Wasn't that the way of life? Laura was the living image of that other luminous beauty, David Mallory's first wife. Paula had never unbent in her dislike of the girl, a dislike that had grown into a steady tension and a masked goading as Laura matured. The advent of a son after three barren years and well into her thirties had been Paula Mallory's greatest triumph. The joy and the intense satisfaction had allowed little room for Laura, though Paula had never been able to drive a wedge between father and daughter, nor between his two children. Laura loved her little stepbrother, and the greatest grief for them both would be to be parted.

'You know she'll deny me Jamie, don't you?' Laura said, and for the first time her voice broke.

'Oh, my dear!' Howard Mitchell had not realised how much contempt he had for Paula Mallory. 'Surely she won't?'

'I'm not to have anything.'

The elderly solicitor tore his eyes away from that suffering young face. 'What do you think people would think if your stepmother treated you badly?'

'I think she hates me too much to care.' Laura's slender hand moved up to her aching temple. 'It's being wrenched away from Jamie that's hurting me so much. He's such a dear little boy, despite Paula's efforts. If she just lets me see Jamie I won't want anything else.'

'I'll speak to her,' Howard said scornfully. 'She hasn't spoken to you yet?'

'No, she's going to make me wait. Even Paula wouldn't tip me out of the house so soon after Father's death, but she's already taken full possession. At the end of the week I'm going to move, which is what she wants. Every instant Jamie and I have together she bitterly resents—cruel, when you think about it. Jamie *is* my stepbrother. He's a lot like Father.' Laura fought the ripple of pain in her throat and conquered it. 'I'll have to sell some of my mother's things.'

'I won't hear of it!' Howard Mitchell stood up, his frail hands clenched tight. 'I'm not a rich man, Laura, but I'm not a poor one either. You must allow Helen and me to help you. Why, we wouldn't have a moment's peace unless you did.'

'Then take Mummy's silver in return. I won't be able to keep it with me, in any case.'

'We'll look after it for you, if that's what you want,' Howard said gruffly. 'Now if I could only find you a good job. . . .'

'It doesn't matter what,' said Laura. 'I like work.'

The solicitor stared down at her intently, his once cornflower blue eyes faded but alert. 'I could almost promise you a job now, but then you mightn't care for it at all.'

Laura's young, tender mouth dropped open with astonishment. 'But I want it, Uncle Howard. I need work.'

'Well, I don't know,' the solicitor switched on a light briskly and sat down. 'You're wonderful with children, in fact I know you'd do the job very successfully, but I keep remembering the sort of life you've had. I know the sort of coldness Paula has always shown towards you, but she never dared order you about. Not when your father was alive.'

'Look, Uncle Howard,' Laura said most definitely, 'what is this about?'

'Would you really mind being a governess?' Howard asked her promptly.

'A governess?' Laura repeated, eyes widening. 'That's a good one!'

'I know.' Howard looked down at the papers on his desk.

'Just a minute now,' Laura leaned forward and caught his hand. 'I didn't say it wouldn't do. Tell me more.'

'A client of mine, head now of a highly respected pastoral family, has the need of a governess for his eight-year-old daughter.'

'Where on earth do they live?' Laura stared at him still somewhat incredulously.

'I can show you a picture of the house,' Howard said dryly. He stood up, went to one of the bookshelves and selected a large, heavy book.

'Good grief, not an historic house?' Laura's silver-grey eyes skimmed the cover.

'Hunter's Moon.' Howard opened the book at a certain page, set it down before Laura and looked at her.

'How stunning,' she said blankly. 'In fact, I adore it.'

'Have you never seen it before in photographs? It's quite a special house.'

'No, I haven't.' Laura was far too honest to pretend. 'It's a very large house, isn't it?'

'A mansion,' Howard Mitchell agreed slowly. 'In the old days, of course, I'm sure they had a team of servants. I'm not sure they don't have them now.'

'I wouldn't be the housekeeper for anything,' Laura commented.

'You're not trying out for that job,' Howard pointed out with just the tiniest, dry laugh. 'Mr Hunter is far from being an ordinary man, and, I feel it my duty to tell you, far from being what we might call an easy man. He's a very powerful individual altogether, a strong, ambitious, highly progressive man. Hunter's Moon today has surpassed even what it was in his father's day. I believe it's one of the top three giant cattle stations in the country, but of course to us city folk it's like some inaccessible, remote kingdom.'

'I don't mind that,' Laura said softly, still staring at the house. 'What kind of woman is his wife?'

'That's just it,' Howard said uncomfortably. 'Though most women would sell their soul for a man like Blaise Hunter, the late Mrs Hunter was killed in an air crash—some say attempting to leave him.'

'What for?' Laura lifted her large, slightly slanted grey eyes.

'Specifically, I think, because the remoteness of the station drove her mad. She was a beautiful, very spoiled girl—Virginia Moorhouse, the heiress. Oh, I know you won't remember, but it was a great society wedding. Blaise insisted that Helen and I be invited. A beautiful girl, but I believe quite difficult from the beginning. The truth of the matter was they weren't all that compatible and poor Virginia couldn't stand the boredom.'

'How appalling!' said Laura, feeling a vast emptiness herself. 'But she had her little girl?'

'There was something sort of . . . peculiar there. I believe though it seems incredible, given Blaise and Virginia, that the child is exceedingly plain. Virginia seemed to regard it as an insult, a kind of humiliation that she should bear an ordinary little girl and not a holy image of herself. Furthermore, though Blaise has never spoken of it, he wanted a son.'

'Exactly,' Laura said rather bitterly. 'A son if it kills you.'

'One needs a son sometimes,' Howard pointed out very gently. 'Only a man could hold a cattle empire together.'

'I suppose so.' Laura clasped the book, feeling

somewhat exhausted. 'Do I understand the property is in the infernal wilds? It only says here South-West Queensland.'

'The Channel Country,' Howard told her. 'A fabulous place. I've only been there once and I've never forgotten. Of course, it was in a good season and the vast desert bloomed.'

'You stayed here?' Laura asked him.

'At Hunter's Moon, yes—a house party for the sake of some celebration or other. You wouldn't believe how they entertain—or did. Blaise has become very hard and withdrawn since Virginia was killed.'

'And why not?' Laura didn't expect to hear anything else. 'So there's only Mr Hunter and his little daughter, who has all of my sympathy so far.'

'Heavens, no!' Howard clasped the edge of his magnificent antique desk. 'The old lady is still alive. Mrs Charlotte Hunter, Blaise's grandmother—a great lady. Then there's Mr and Mrs Steven Hunter. Steven is Blaise's younger brother, a very pleasant man, but from what I hear he won't make even the smallest decision without Blaise to confirm it. Then there's Mrs Steven Hunter's sister—I can't think of her name, something exotic—she finds plenty of reasons for staying. I'm only telling you all this because I feel bound to and I know you're very discreet. I couldn't let you go off, if you chose to, without putting you in the picture.'

Laura waited a few moments, although she had already made up her mind. 'Well, I know I'll be comfortable unless they lock me up in the maids' quarters, but what about the money?'

'Excellent,' Howard said.

'Then that's it.' Although there were all sorts of unbearable griefs in her Laura knew she had to get away. In a few days' time Paula would show what she was really made of, so any kind of position was really being forced on her. Why not this one? She could arrange to continue her studies externally.

'Don't be in a hurry to make up your mind,' Howard told her. 'I don't know for certain, but I don't think it's a happy house.'

'I'll be helping somebody, won't I?' Laura asked. 'I want to be nice to that little girl. You've told me she's plain, do you know anything at all about her behaviour or what stage she's at with her lessons?'

'It's so difficult to actually *ask* Blaise,' Howard said almost timidly. 'All I know is he considers her too young to send away to boarding school. He doesn't want just any young girl to give her company. He has very specific requirements—sound background, young lady, educated, that type of thing. I'm not sure you fit the bill. I'm not sure at all.'

'Uncle Howard!' Laura burst out, astonished.

'How shall I put this?' the solicitor mused. 'Governesses base their success, I should think, on being kind, competent and able to hold the attention of children. They wouldn't be required, I should imagine, to be completely beautiful.'

'I'm not that, Uncle Howard.' A smile relieved the tension in the muscles of Laura's face.

'Take it from me, my dear, you are,' the elderly solicitor said seriously. 'Good looks, at times, can be a severe disadvantage.'

'Oh, goodness!' All at once Laura felt crushed and very tired. 'This isn't the classic romance situation, is it? Too-pretty governess, master of the house, glowering female relatives and sundry admirers?'

'Women, I've found, generally like their plainer sisters better.'

'Blast!' Laura said violently. Just one glance at a

house and she had let herself be seduced.

'I'm merely stating facts. How do I know, for instance, that some female out there might not see you as a threat? Blaise Hunter is a striking-looking man. He's also very rich and influential.'

'I don't believe I would be interested.'

'You'll have to stick to that,' Howard said unexpectedly. 'Unhappiness can make men cruel, even good men. Blaise Hunter doesn't have to ask anything of women. They just throw themselves at his feet.'

'How boring!' Laura declared dryly. 'I expect he hates them for that reason. Let me say, Uncle Howard, truly at this moment I have no room in my life for an unrequited passion. I know the hazards involved and I would still like the job.'

'My case rests,' Howard said in a quiet voice without mockery. 'I daresay you can play down your looks a little and tie back that lovely hair. At least until you get the feel of the place.'

'Surely someone from the household will be speaking to me?' Laura asked him.

'My dear, they're a thousand miles away, except Blaise, and he has left it entirely up to me.' Howard Mitchell leaned back in his deep comfortable armchair and sighed. 'That your father should do this to you!'

'He gave me a great deal.'

'I'm conscious of that,' Howard said quietly, 'but I'm saddened nevertheless. What I can't understand is he drew up that last will without me.'

'Perhaps he knew you would try to alter it.'

'What family solicitor wouldn't?'

'It doesn't matter now, Uncle Howard,' Laura said. 'I'm quite sure one can be happy without money, though I'm not so sure one can be happy without one's loved ones. I'm going to miss Jamie dreadfully.'

'Don't expect the worst, dear,' said Howard.

The grey phone on his desk rang and he picked up the receiver. 'Yes, Miss Stafford?' His secretary's voice spoke at the other end of the intercom and Howard Mitchell's lips came together in involuntary astonishment. 'Good heavens!' He glanced up sharply and looked at Laura, who was registering his surprise. 'Give me one moment and I'll be there.'

The receiver went down and Howard spoke in hushed tones. 'Speak of the devil!'

'One of your clients?' Laura found the heart to smile.

Howard was still looking intensely startled. 'It's Blaise Hunter.'

Instantly Laura rose to her feet. 'Don't you want to see him?'

'Of course—I always have done. It's just that it's so unexpected. I know this visit was made in great haste. Securing a governess for his daughter was only a small item on his agenda.'

'I think I'll be getting myself along,' Laura said wryly, 'or do you want me to face him now?'

Howard hesitated uncertainly. 'Something's bothering me about all this. I'd like to have time to think. For *you* to have time. You don't have to rush into anything, and furthermore, I won't let you.'

'At least I'll get a glimpse of the great man.' Laura's fine-boned face had tightened fastidiously. She stood straight, a taller than average girl, her slenderness only recently honed to fragility. The light gleamed on her white-gold hair and along the lines of her simple white silk dress. In no way did she look bitter or resentful or deprived as she had perhaps every right to be. Neither did she look the picture of one who played traditionally a modest and unassuming role. She looked a beautiful, vulnerable young girl, and her whole appearance proclaimed a moneyed background. Up until now.

Howard got up quickly to join her. 'All right, my dear, go home to Helen. She's expecting you for dinner and afterwards we can talk.'

At the open doorway he patted her shoulder, and as she turned the smallest step Laura had her first glimpse of Blaise Hunter. It shocked her and made her feel things she had never felt before; a kind of fear and antagonism. He was, quite simply, unlike any man she had ever seen before. Handsome, certainly, in a black-haired, black-eyed, hawk-faced style, arrogance in every bone, but when it came down to it, it wasn't the handsomeness that caught her, the height and breadth of shoulder, but the aura. He had a quality, a magnetism, that was alive.

She heard him speak to Uncle Howard and the voice was the affirmation of the aura. She would be quite insane to come within the orbit of this man, because no matter what Uncle Howard said about him, the praises he sang, here was a man who knew how to make a woman suffer. Probably he would keep them suffering all his life.

Laura didn't stop, yet she felt him glance at her. His skin was scorched to the deepest tan, yet it was clean and polished. There was no weight on him anywhere, but the power was there, muscle rippling beneath the elegant city clothes. His eyes were brilliant, yet cold and glittering, a searching, cynical gaze that missed nothing, the apprehension and barely veiled antipathy he had drawn up so effortlessly. He did not need words or actions to see the stress in Laura, and with his glance on her she felt too weak to turn away.

It was an odd moment when words, introductions seemed required. Howard Mitchell, watching them both, not without some feeling of dismay, thought Laura was locked like a statue. He knew she wanted to flee just as he knew she couldn't. It was an acknowledgment of Blaise Hunter's power, an arrestment of her own will.

In the end, Blaise took the initiative out of his hands. 'This young lady looks familiar,' he said, rather brusquely.

'My dear Blaise, I don't think you've ever seen Laura before.'

'No?' The black eyes slashed back over Laura's face. 'Surely you have a photograph of her—next to that sculpture you brought back from your travels?'

'Good lord!' Howard smiled awkwardly. Did that coal-black glance miss anything? He saw, as he turned to Laura, that she had partially recovered her usual lovely poise, so he made the introductions solemnly as though they were of great importance.

Tall as she was, Laura felt precariously small as Blaise Hunter stood over her, and though she gave him her hand she did not give him a smile.

'It seems to me I should remember something about you, Miss Mallory?' He didn't spare her the mockery when he noticed how quickly she withdrew her hand.

'I don't think so, Mr Hunter. I'm totally unmemorable.'

If Laura needed a job she wasn't going about it the right way. Now that the situation was laid before Howard he was certain that he must speak now if Laura was to secure this post at all. He was sure, like Laura, that Paula Mallory would deny her stepdaughter a home, and Laura, to keep her pride and her confidence, desperately needed a job and a breathing space.

'Do come inside, both of you,' he said with his habitual kindliness, leaning back against the closed door of his office as they both stood inside on the wide expanse of Persian carpet. 'Sit down, sit down,' he began, and smiled at them. 'Probably you may have read, Blaise, that Laura's father died recently. David Mallory of Mallory and Sunderland, the structural engineers?'

'Of course,' the hawk face tightened. 'My condolences, Miss Mallory.'

'Thank you.' It was the first bit of sincerity he had shown.

'An unhappy story all round.' Howard looked towards Laura to see if he had her permission to go on, and just as it seemed she would prefer anything to working for Blaise Hunter very slightly she nodded her head. 'The thing is, Blaise, I think I may have found the ideal solution for you and for Laura. Laura feels the need of a breathing space, a change of habitat—this has been a profoundly upsetting experience for her, so I took the liberty of discussing your need of a governess with her.'

'Miss Mallory? My dear Howard!' There was a nice inflection of amusement and scorn in the dark voice.

'Why ever not?' Howard asked mildly, his blue glance unfocused as he took off his glasses for a moment.

'Well, it's a very charming idea, of course,' a black sidelong glance at Laura's silk-clothed figure, 'but Miss Mallory is the most unlikely-looking governess I've ever seen.'

'Because I'm pretty?' Her dawn-soft eyes actually flashed at him.

'You're not *pretty*, Miss Mallory,' he said dryly, 'and please don't lose your sense of humour.'

'I'm in rather desperate need of a job, Mr Hunter,' she said quietly, and a flame of quick colour burned on her fine cheekbones.

'David Mallory's daughter?' He leaned back in his chair, the very picture of superiority and arrogance.

'You mustn't hurt Laura,' Howard Mitchell said very earnestly. 'This is painful for me to say and doubly painful for Laura the need of my saying it, but Laura was not mentioned in her father's will.'

'I suppose some fortune-hunter was making an ass of himself over her?' Blaise Hunter exclaimed bluntly.

'I don't think we need explain anything more to Mr Hunter, Uncle Howard,' Laura said tonelessly, and came gracefully to her feet. 'I'll go on home now, shall I?'

'Touching! Young pride.' From his relaxed position in the armchair Blaise Hunter looked up at her. 'Do sit down again, Miss Mallory. I'm very sorry to hear you've been disinherited, but I'm sure a beautiful girl such as yourself would have no need to bury herself in the wilderness. The city would seem the answer, with all its opportunities.'

'Such as?' At that moment Laura could conceive of no one she could hate more.

'I love the brilliant marriage bit, don't you? It should be easy for a girl with your style.'

'Blaise, Blaise!' Howard Mitchell murmured unhappily, knowing he couldn't allow this kind of confrontation to continue. Laura, with her shining blonde beauty, had come too close to the bitterness that was in him—a bitterness he had never forgotten.

Unexpectedly, against the leashed cruelty, Laura's clear young voice was quite gentle. 'May I tell you a secret, Mr Hunter?' she confided. 'Apart from Uncle Howard, I don't think I've ever known a really *nice* man in my life. I do not want any man I can't place all my faith in and trust.'

'Certainly then you'll be an old maid.' Now the vibrant voice went soft with mockery. 'Extraordinary as it may seem to you, Miss Mallory, I used to feel like that once, but everyone comes to reality sooner or later. There *is* no perfect trust between man and woman.'

'Could there not be between woman and child? I'd like to help your daughter.'

'Sit down,' he said curtly, his eyes touching on her too-slender standing body. 'Why do you really want this job?' Blaise Hunter waved an imperious hand as the elderly solicitor tried to intervene. 'Are you on the run from someone—you know, a lover?'

'I. . . .' Laura was so angry, she choked.

'Then the answer is no.'

'Just a minute, Mr Hunter,' she spread her hand out to stop him. 'I don't think I want this job at all.'

'Be sensible,' he jeered at her. 'You're not afraid of the Outback, the vastness or the utter remoteness?'

She gave a funny little laugh, a laugh that was wrenched from her. 'I've never been Outback.'

'What did you say?' His voice was flat and drawling.

'To tell the truth, I've always wanted to go, but there hasn't been the time. I had a few months in the U.K. and Europe, and the rest of the time I've been at university.'

'Really, Howard,' Blaise Hunter looked across at the somewhat nervous solicitor, 'I've no doubt you consider Miss Mallory is someone special, but I don't give a damn about her pretty speech and her beauty. She's hopeless whichever way you look at it.'

'You know what I think, Mr Hunter,' Laura began ominously.

'Something about you bothers me?' He looked at her and laughed. 'Quite right. Enough to make me downright rude. I know your type of woman, Miss Mallory, and quite frankly I only consider them decoration.'

'You really are a total. . . .'

'I know.' For the first time he smiled at her and almost audibly Laura sucked in her breath. There would be plenty of women who wouldn't care how cruel he was as long as he smiled like that.

'Forgive us, Blaise, for wasting your time,' Howard Mitchell interrupted suavely. 'I'm sure I can find you a girl as ugly as sin.'

'Oh well, you know how it is,' Blaise said, and gave the solicitor that same brilliant smile. 'Miss Mallory must hear enough nice things every day of her life.'

'And she deserves every one of them. It might be difficult to find the right girl as quickly as you want. Laura here, of course, has every qualification. . . .'

'She shouldn't boast about it.'

'Please, Blaise. . . .'

'I'm sorry, Howard, I didn't mean to criticise. She is undoubtedly a cultured young woman and well educated, but is she, for example, any good with kids?'

'A natural,' Howard announced. 'Why, Laura has a young brother.'

'Please, Uncle Howard. . . .' Laura was unprepared for the storm of emotion that welled up in her. She had no right to her brother any more. No right to her home, to the old way of life. Didn't *anyone* see that? The tears rushed into her eyes so that she was blinded by them. She stood up. She didn't care. She was not capable of taking any more suffering now. Father, Father, how could you *do* this to me. . . .

'What is it?' Strong hands caught and held her just above the elbow.

She shook her head and tried to blink the tears away

to restore her vision. This man had no right to humiliate her, to touch her. He was holding her so tightly it was pain.

'My dear little girl!' Howard Mitchell, too, came to her, his silver eyebrows working with distress. 'That I should have done this to you! I never thought.'

'Do you mind, Mr Hunter? You're hurting me.' Laura finally lifted her head.

'You gave me the impression if I hadn't held you, you'd have fallen down.' His voice wasn't gentle, but even a little savage.

'All I can offer in excuse is I'm tired and I'm hungry. . . .'

'And you're as unhappy as hell.'

'Yes.' She knew he had recognised that from the beginning. 'May I go now?'

'Not with that tragic face,' he said brusquely. 'You may flatter yourself you've moved me. Allow me to buy you dinner.'

She was afraid if she stayed another minute she would tell him she hated him. 'I'll say goodbye, Uncle Howard,' she whispered.

'Do you know it's raining outside,' Blaise Hunter told her bluntly. 'You'll get drenched.'

'A storm, no more.' Her arms were still smarting where he had held her.

'Blaise, I haven't even asked you what you wanted to consult me about,' Howard said distractedly, thinking the atmosphere was seething far more inside than out.

'I've forgotten. What you were doing about the governess. We might have dinner, something like that.' The black eyes were still resting on Laura's silver-fair downbent head. 'It astonishes me that so poised a young lady should burst into tears.'

'Only because you don't know the full story, Blaise,'

Howard Mitchell said quietly. 'Why don't we all go home to dinner? I'll just put a call through to Helen. She'll be delighted to see you, Blaise.'

At this Laura lifted her head swiftly, her tear-washed eyes sparkling radiantly in the light. 'Nor for me, thank you, Uncle Howard. Another time.'

'Well, that's wonderful!' Blaise Hunter exclaimed dryly. 'Miss Mallory is being rude. Is it so strange that I might wish to know about a young woman who seeks employment in my home?'

Laura was all too aware of her tear-stained face, but she turned to face him. 'You don't like me, Mr Hunter, nor indeed anything about me. Why don't we let it go at that?'

'Why don't we?' He shrugged his powerful shoulders and turned away from her, speaking to the solicitor. 'Is this heroic stand real?'

'Of course it is.' Howard Mitchell was not so much displeased as saddened. 'It would be better for you, my boy, if you could acknowledge that women *are* heroic.'

'They haven't crowded *my* life. Only my grandmother was proud and strong enough to accept her fate and revel in it.'

'A wonderful woman,' Howard seconded sincerely. 'A great lady.'

Blaise Hunter made no further comment but walked to the phone. 'Surely it's time to close up? What's your number again? I want to surprise Helen.'

Howard, looking pleased, gave it to him and as he began to dial turned away to speak to Laura. 'Do come home with us, my dear. Blaise is a fine man when you get to know him.'

'I'm sorry, Uncle Howard,' she answered, just as quietly, 'but he seems more like a man to stay away from.'

'You don't want the job?'

'I thought I wanted it, but it's perfectly obvious Mr Hunter hates women. Furthermore, I'm not going to allow him to insult *me*.'

'Yes, it has been antagonism at first sight, but you don't have to think about it now. Our home is yours and big enough for all of us. Helen will be upset that you're not coming.'

'She'll understand.'

After a few moments Blaise Hunter hung up the phone and walked to a wall cabinet, holding up Laura's photograph and looking at it. 'You're very photogenic, Miss Mallory,' he said smoothly. 'I'm sorry I can't offer you the position of governess for my daughter, but I'm afraid you'd find yourself worse off than you are now.'

'I believe you, Mr Hunter,' she answered quietly, offering the sacrilege of talking back.

When he swung around on her there was even a sparkle of laughter in his eyes. 'You may not believe this, Miss Mallory, but I'm definitely being kind to you—fairly rare these days. Howard will find me some nice, modest young woman who'll fit in well and be prepared to suffer solitude.'

'I certainly hope he will,' Laura said blindly, 'for your daughter's sake. You haven't mentioned her once.'

All the way out to her home, now Paula's, Blaise Hunter addressed his remarks to Howard, without once glancing back at Laura or including her in the conversation. Laura didn't care. She sat in the back of Howard's Daimler feeling sickened inside. In happier days she would have been in a fury of resentment at Blaise Hunter's harsh and uncompromisingly chauvinistic attitude, but everything seemed to be conspiring

to shatter her. She could barely face the thought of
Paula inside.

When they pulled up outside the vine-encrusted
gates of the big Tudor-style house Paula had so desired
Howard turned to speak to her and Blaise Hunter got
out of the car to open her door.

'Ring me in the morning, dear,' Howard said.

'Yes.' The tension that was slowly gnawing at her
showed in the almost breakable posture of her body
and the strain on her young face. 'Goodbye, Mr
Hunter,' she said, raising her face.

'Goodbye, Miss Mallory,' he said abruptly. 'No
one as innocent as you should get their fingers
burned.'

CHAPTER TWO

As she let herself in the front door, Jamie came hurtling
down the stairway to meet her.

'I knew it was you as soon as I saw Uncle Howard's
car!' He held out his hands to her and Laura caught
them, lowering herself to his level and kissing his
sweetly scented four-year-old cheek.

'You've had your bath.'

'Yes, and I dropped things all over the floor. It made
a noise like thunder. Did you get caught in the storm?'

'No, look—I'm all nice and dry.'

'Why didn't Uncle Howard come in?' Jamie asked.
'I like him, and he always has something nice for me
in his pocket.'

'He was busy tonight, darling,' Laura explained.

'Oh.' Immediately Jamie lost interest. 'You have to

help me with my puzzle—I've done it all wrong.'

Laura stood up and they continued to hold hands. How I love him, Laura thought. How I love Paula's child. Overnight life had turned into a great big mess.

'Oh, you're home, Laura.' A plump, pleasant-faced woman in her late fifties came into the hallway, beaming first at Jamie, a handsome little blond boy, then at his equally well endowed stepsister. 'I hope you're not going to tell me you're not hungry.'

'As a matter of fact, I am.' With Jamie clinging lovingly to her hand Laura felt a resurgence of life.

'Good!' Jean Frazer, their housekeeper, said with satisfaction.

'Jean's made you something lovely,' said Jamie. 'It has chicken in it and she let me taste it. I want to stay with you while you have your tea.'

'Is Mrs Mallory in?' Laura asked the housekeeper in her gentle voice.

'No, dear,' Jean Frazer answered dryly. 'That friend of hers, Mrs Carroll, has asked her to stay on to dinner. She did say she wouldn't be late.'

'I see.' Tenderly Laura ruffled Jamie's silky fair hair. 'What say we eat in the kitchen tonight?'

'I think we should all the time,' Jamie answered, seriously. 'It would be less bother. Why can't I get a rabbit? Chris at pre-school has a pet rabbit—a white one.'

Over the delicious meal Jean had so lovingly prepared the little boy kept the two women laughing at all the events of his day, both at pre-school and at home. Extraordinarily his father's death had not altered his behaviour in any way, for in actual fact his deepest feelings and relationship were tied up with his stepsister, who always found time for him and was never frantically busy and forever going out in the evening.

'Bedtime for you, my boy!' Laura announced about seven o'clock. 'I've noticed all those little yawns.'

'Read me to sleep, Laura,' he urged her, examining with satisfaction the correctly pieced together jigsaw puzzle. 'The one about the little yellow car on the boat dock.'

'Yes, that is an interesting one,' she replied.

Less than ten minutes later she was downstairs again, making her way to the luxurious big kitchen where Jean was loading the dishwasher.

'Fast asleep, is he?' Jean asked.

'And happy.'

'Happy now.' Jean sniffed. 'What's he going to do if you leave here?'

'I'll see him all the time.'

'Oh, come on!' Jean straightened up, her plump cheeks flushed. 'We can't pretend to ourselves, love.'

'No.' Laura looked down sightlessly at the shining, stainless steel twin sinks. 'I'll go to pieces, Jean, when it happens.'

'I expect I'll have a few words to say too. I'm leaving. As soon as you do, so do I.'

'But you *can't*!' Laura moved forward and caught the older woman's arm. 'Jamie needs you, Jean. He loves you. You're so kind and so good and so comfortable. He can't lose both of us.'

'He has his mother,' said Jean, but it was easy to see she was shaken.

'Paula *is* his mother,' Laura agreed, 'but she's in and out all the time. She hasn't resumed her social life yet, but it will come, and who's to look after Jamie then?'

'I daresay another good, kind woman.'

'You can't do it, Jean,' Laura protested.

'It will be a pretty day when you leave this house,'

said Jean, her homely face expressing condemnation.

'I'll survive, Jean. Others have had to face the same experience.'

'Name them,' Jean burst out belligerently. 'Not only will your little brother miss you unbearably, I will too. Ten years I've been with you. Your mamma hired me, God rest her soul. Now Mr Mallory has gone. Perhaps it's time for me to go too. Your stepmother can find herself another wonderful cook.'

'It's Jamie,' Laura explained, and brushed a hand over her eyes.

'Yes, it's Jamie,' Jean answered, then stopped abruptly. 'Your stepmother can only do this because she's not a church person. Something new came into this family with her. She changed your father.'

'He chose to be changed.'

'I can't believe that will!' Jean flared up again with hostility. 'Your father would never do *that* to you.'

'He gave me a lot, Jean,' Laura reminded her. 'We had lots of wonderful times.'

'Yes, and I know when they were.' Jean ran and snatched up a tablecloth and began to rub at the shining sink. 'How can Mrs Mallory face the world if she turns you out of your own home? How could she face your father's friends if she split up his two children?'

Laura walked away and looked out the window. The sky had cleared and it was full of stars. 'Paula will find a perfectly plausible story to tell them.'

'And no one will believe it. She was indeed fortunate to have two friends of hers around when your father made that new will.'

'I think discussing this any more, Jean, will only upset us. In addition, it won't do a scrap of good.'

'And what about Mr Mitchell, then? Don't tell me he's going to take this so well. Why, he and Mrs

Mitchell are as fond of you as if you were their own granddaughter. It seems inconceivable that Mr Mallory would have acted without him. They were friends for so long, and Mr Mitchell would have argued your case, your birthright. I tell you, the whole thing has me so mad I don't really think I can stay in this house feeling as I do. It's inhuman to leave you a beggar and that woman rich!'

'It will all come to Jamie, that's the point,' said Laura.

'By all means Jamie must get his share, but so must you. I feel so indignant I could *burst*!'

'Hush, Jean!' Laura took the woman's arm and patted it. 'Maybe everything has turned out differently from what we hoped and expected, but I'm twenty years old.'

'Just twenty—a great age!'

'Old enough, certainly, to get a job.'

'If it comes to that,' Jean said hardily, 'I have money for you to continue your studies. In fact I have a nice little nest egg set aside.'

It was too much for Laura. She made a piteous little sound and tried to hide her face in the crook of her arm like a bird with a broken wing.

'There, lovey, *there!*' Motherly Jean made a swoop for her. 'Did you really think I was going to stand by and do nothing?'

'Oh, Jean, Jean!' Laura muttered between heart-broken sobs.

'Do let me do it, love—and no need to thank me. You do know I've always been so proud of you—a clever girl. I never had any brains myself.'

'Just unlimited kindness.' Laura drew her hand away from her eyes, frightened now that if she didn't stop, she would be unable to. 'First Uncle Howard, then you.'

'You've got friends,' Jean maintained stoutly. 'True friends to stand by you.'

'And it makes me very happy, but *I* can't dip into your savings, Jean. Who knows when you may need them? Besides, I'm perfectly capable of finding a job.'

'But your degree, don't you want it?'

'Oh yes, Jean, I want it.' Laura was aghast at the misery on Jean's dear, familiar face, 'and I'll get it too. I'm not the only student who's had to finish a course at night or externally.'

'But you've only a year to go.' Jean's eyes behind her blue-rimmed glasses were moist.

'It will all work out. Don't worry, Jean,' Laura said gently. 'If you must know, I don't think I deserve your goodness.'

'That you do,' Jean said loudly, and punched the back of a chair. 'Nothing will be any good in this house without you. Not for me. Not for Jamie.'

Many hours later, Laura at last fell asleep, and when she awoke in the morning and went down to breakfast Paula greeted her with the familiar, derisory note in her voice.

'Up at last, Laura?'

'I don't have a class until this afternoon.'

'Oh, yes. What it is to be a university student!' There was definite warning in the tone, like the crackling of fire along a fuse. 'I think you should remember I don't intend to pay any more money out on your education.'

'I'm not asking you to, Paula,' Laura said quietly, grateful for Jean's sudden appearance with her breakfast.

'There, Laura,' Jean said warmly. 'Juice, fruit, and I've made you some nice scrambled egg. You must get your protein.'

'Of course,' Paula agreed mockingly. 'Thank you, Jean. I would like to speak to Miss Mallory.' The tone of Paula's husky voice was harsh and final, and Laura could well see how Jean might not be persuaded to stay. Paula, given power, was a natural bully, just as Laura would always remain gracious.

'I think the time has come,' Paula announced, 'for us to arrive at some settlement. Now that your father has gone there's nothing we have in common.'

'Except Jamie.' The cold pineapple juice slid down Laura's parched throat.

'Jamie is *my* son!' Paula burst out with sudden excitement. 'I know you've done everything in your power to steal his affection.'

'That's ridiculous, Paula.' Laura hid her shaking hands. 'Jamie and I are brother and sister. It's natural for us to love one another.'

'You've made an issue of it to undermine me. I pointed this out many times to your father, and finally he had to take it very seriously indeed.'

'You spoke to Father?' Laura cried, her shock so great she thought she would faint. 'You complained to Father about me?'

'But how young you are, Laura!' Paula said contemptuously. 'I *had* to and I *wanted* to. I didn't intend to take second place to you, make no mistake.'

'I would have thought there was room enough for all of us.' She couldn't eat now, not with Paula looking at her with hatred. When her father had first brought Paula home, even though she had been on her best behaviour, Paula had irresistibly reminded her of the Wicked Queen in *Snow White*. Paula had raven-dark hair that grew in a widow's peak, she had icy blue eyes and a very white skin. She was a handsome woman, then and now, but Laura had always thought it a destructive beauty. She was showing the cruel side to her now.

'That would be asking the impossible,' Paula gave a ragged laugh. 'Jamie and I can get along without you very well. Just as your father could. He was putty in my hands.'

Laura looked at her but said nothing.

'Oh, go on, go on, give me that big, martyred stare. Such is the way men are. After I had Jamie I could ask anything of your father, and I did. It wasn't easy to win him around entirely, but in the end I did. Daughters must be allowed to marry. Sons must inherit.'

'I don't think I'm giving you an argument, Paula,' Laura said.

'Of course not, that's why I hate you—you're so damned unbelievable. Anyone else with so much money involved would be mounting a case.' The long, frozen blue eyes narrowed. 'Or are you? Is that stuffed shirt old Mitchell talking of contesting the will?'

'He seems to think we would get a favourable judgment.' Laura decided to turn the tables.

'Is he crazy?' Paula stared at her. 'The will is airtight!'

'Then why look so worried?'

'Don't talk back to me, miss,' Paula snapped angrily. 'If you crawl on your hands and knees I might give you something.'

Laura threw down her table napkin. 'I won't do that, Paula, under any circumstances. I take it you want me to leave?'

'In fact, my dear, I can't wait.' Paula stretched out her hand towards fresh coffee. 'Why don't you marry Brett Hartley? A girl in your position might be expected to jump at the chance.'

'I guess I'd rather make my own way in life.'

'You're wonderful!' sneered Paula. 'So wonderful it makes me sick. I think it would be easier to like you if you were a real bitch.'

'That's right,' Laura stood up, 'but since I'm not, you're left with a lot to celebrate. I hope you're going to allow me to see Jamie?'

'You expect it?' Paula looked up with an odd smile.

'I hope for it.'

'But the answer is no. I can take very good care of my son myself. It would be preferable for him to forget you at once. Little children have short memories. You notice there were no floods of tears for his father.'

'It hasn't really sunk in,' Laura said. 'He thinks his daddy is on one of those long trips again—or that's how he's coping with it in his mind.'

'If you love Jamie,' Paula gave her peculiar, tight smile, 'you'll make no attempt to see him after you've left here. It would be *so* unsettling.'

'Not half so unsettling as losing the sister he loves.'

'He'll get used to the idea very quickly.'

'You're foolish if you believe that, Paula. And stupid. You deprive me of Jamie and I will contest the will. Furthermore, I stand a good chance of winning. Into the bargain I'll see to it that every friend you and Father ever had—and I mean the people you *love* to be seen with—knows exactly what kind of woman you are; a woman who claimed *everything*. . . .'

'For Jamie, my *son!*' Paula shouted, moving her right hand so violently she sent her half-filled coffee cup over. 'You mean behind that lily-pure exterior is a filthy little bitch!' she cried hysterically.

'Of course.' Laura's lustrous eyes had a crusading flame. 'People do many things in the name of love, but

I can't seem to do much for myself. Perhaps I'm so
numb that Father didn't love me enough to leave me
anything, even a remembrance, a reminder. He told
me once he loved us equally, Jamie and me, but of
course I always knew he loved Jamie more. It never
bothered me. You see, I too love him so much I'm
going to fight you for his happiness. Not my own. *His*.
If there's *some* good in you, you won't let that happen.
All I want is to see Jamie at the weekend. I won't
bother you and I won't come here, except to collect
him, but I do want him to know he has me and that I
love him very much.'

'You insolent slut!' Paula's face was stretched so
tightly it looked as if the bones would slash through
the skin. 'Get out of here, and go quickly! I can't bear
to look at you another second.'

'Thank you, Paula,' Laura said quietly. 'I'll have my
things out by tonight and I'll let you know when I
want to see Jamie.'

Paula stopped thinking rationally. She leapt to her
feet, trembling, her thin, almost breastless body clearly
outlined beneath the thin cloth of her housecoat. 'Over
my dead body,' she cried fiercely. Had she a whip in
her hands she would have lashed out in a frenzy, but
Laura stood close to her with absolutely no fear.

'Don't underestimate me, Paula,' she said. 'I guess
we all want to fight clean, but nobility can be too ex-
pensive. I know Jamie needs me. I *know* this. I can't
make it easy for you and myself and abandon him.
Whatever else Father wanted he never wanted that.'

She knew Paula was beaten, if only in that moment,
for her stepmother fell back limply into the chair. 'Get
out, Laura,' she said hollowly. 'Go to your room and
stay there until I've dressed and taken Jamie out. Don't
attempt to see or torment him. You have all day to

make your arrangements, but be out of here by to-night.'

An hour later only a white-faced Laura and a desper-ately flushed Jean were left in the house.

'I could kill her!' Jean was saying, down on the floor wildly searching for a shoe.

'I've got it,' Laura said wearily. 'I'm unhappy!'

'I'd say you had a right to be. This is the most ter-rible thing I've heard of in all my life. What kind of a man *was* your father? I worked for him for years and found him perfectly all right. Yet he's done this to you, the gentlest little soul.'

'Not so gentle,' Laura said wryly. 'Gentle because I didn't have to be anything else. Maybe I'm a fool and I should contest the will, but Paula would make it ugly and everyone would know everything about us all. Maybe, too, I don't really want to admit to myself, let alone the whole world, that Father didn't want to leave me anything. I suppose he thought I would get married sooner or later or he would be around for a long time....' Laura sank down on the bed and looked straight ahead. 'I'd better forget it. I won't be out of here if I don't.'

'So where are you going?' Jean asked with the vio-lence of helplessness.

'I've got friends,' said Laura, and gave a peculiar little smile. 'I'll ring Uncle Howard in a moment, but I really don't like upsetting him. He suffers from high blood pressure, and he's always been hostile towards Paula.'

Outside in the upstairs hallway the phone rang and Jean came jerkily to her feet. 'That's probably him now.' When she returned in a minute she seemed oddly excited. 'A Mr Hunter on the line.'

'It happens to all of us,' Laura threw herself backwards on the bed, 'the last straw to break the camel's back.'

'Come on, Laura,' Jean said sharply. 'Answer him. Despite what you told me, he may have changed his mind.'

'And who the devil cares!'

'Up!' Jean ordered sternly. 'He might be the answer to a prayer.'

That set Laura laughing, a hilarity approaching a storm of tears.

'Good morning, Mr Hunter,' she said, her voice bright and empty.

'How nice of you to answer, Miss Mallory.'

'I was told to,' Laura shrugged.

'I hope I'm not disturbing you.'

'Not at all. I'm moving out.'

'How soul-destroying!'

'It is rather.' Surprisingly the deep, sardonic voice was restoring her balance. Sympathy and she would have gone to pieces.

'I suppose you have somewhere to go?' he queried.

'You surprise me, Mr Hunter—betraying so much interest.' Jean had stepped out into the hallway now, standing ponderously and unashamedly behind her.

'I guess I'm as drearily human as the rest of us,' the dark voice murmured in self-mockery. 'Apparently you haven't the wits to ask why I'm ringing?'

'I don't know that I care,' she answered, not altogether truthfully.

'Oh well, undoubtedly you will. I had the absurd idea that you were an extremely cherished young lady, but it seems you're not.'

'There must be a few things in life you don't know about, Mr Hunter.'

'Nothing I'm not interested in,' he returned arrogantly. '*You* interest me, Miss Mallory—a well bred, well brought up young lady without any visible means of support.'

'Temporarily.'

'And perhaps unnecessarily. Ruthless as you no doubt think me, I don't like to see *any* woman helpless. If your position is so precarious the best way out of the dilemma would be for you to leave with me.'

Laura, standing so straightly, suddenly slid to the floor without dropping the phone.

'Are you there, Miss Mallory?' He didn't even raise his voice.

'Uncle Howard has been talking to you,' she said flatly.

'Of course. Helen too. They quite swept me away.'

'They're my friends.'

'They are,' he agreed.

It was all too much for Laura to take in at once, to decide. 'I can't think, Mr Hunter,' she said shakily into the phone. 'I can't even talk. I have to be out of here by tonight.'

'The devil you do!' he said roughly. 'What kind of woman is your stepmother?'

'Very pleasant to a lot of people,' Laura said. 'It's just that she doesn't like me.' There was simply nothing more to say. Without waiting for one of his sardonic comments she replaced the receiver and looked up Jean, who was leaning over her positively avidly.

'What was all that talk?'

Laura let her blonde head fall back against the wall. 'I think it meant he's offering me the job.'

'Then take it, dear, for a little while. Take it and get away from here.'

'I can't go and leave Jamie,' Laura protested.

'Mrs Mallory will beat you,' said Jean. 'She'll take the boy travelling. She'll love it, and so might he. *You* won't be able to stop her.'

'She has to come home some time.'

'Aye, she does, but she has a lot of clout on her side. She's the boy's mother. We both know between the two of us we've mothered him, but she has the all-powerful claim.'

'I'll contest the will,' Laura declared.

'Do it, but it might take ages. You've been deeply hurt by all this. Cure yourself out there in the Outback. Give yourself a little time. It's a whole new world, surely you're curious about it?'

'No,' Laura said sombrely, 'the thought of leaving Jamie is killing me. For four years he's been the light of my life.'

'There's an answer somewhere!' Jean cried distractedly. 'I've prayed to the good Lord. Then this man's voice on the telephone this morning. He sounds like a man of consequence, a man to be reckoned with—I don't know. I only know I felt some flood of gratitude. I'm a bit psychic, as you know.'

Laura started to laugh again and the sound of it was vaguely worrying. 'You're wrong more often than you're right, Jean,' she reminded the other woman.

'Well I couldn't stand to be right all the time. Get up, love, there's a good girl.' The mock-indignant voice gentled. 'So how did you leave it?'

'I hung up on him,' said Laura, rising. 'Let's get with it, Jean, packing.'

'Why let her push you out?' Jean muttered. 'Ignore her and go in your own time.'

'I must go, Jean.' Laura looked fragile enough to be

breakable, the gleaming mass of her hair moving across her face. 'Just don't tell me you're going too. Jamie would be bereft.'

It was thirty minutes later when they were startled by the sound of a car sweeping up the drive.

'What's that?' they asked one another, riveted by the thought that it might be Paula.

Laura seemed incapable of movement, so Jean walked to the window. 'It's Mr Mitchell. That's his Daimler.'

Instantly Laura was mobilised. 'Remember, now, don't tell him about the argument.'

'All the same, he'll know,' Jean answered, going on with the packing.

Laura flew down the stairway and threw open the front door, the warmth in her face dying when she saw who stood outside the pedimented doorway. Her body seemed to snap and she slumped. 'Mr Hunter.'

'I'm enchanted by your disappointment.' He spoke as he always did, mockingly.

'I thought it was Uncle Howard.' She made an effort to bring the strength back into her body.

'Nevertheless, you have an ally. Are you going to let me in, or must I be anchored to the front stairs?'

There was nothing else to do except show him into the drawing room, conscious that he was watching her with very deliberate attention. So she was untidy, shoeless. It could not have meant less to her. She even found joy in it, seeing he was so contemptuous of a woman's beauty.

'Your stepmother is not at home?' he looked around the room, then back at her.

'Would you like to meet her?'

'As a matter of fact, I would.' There was no wryness, no amusement in his face, but a ruthless austerity. He walked to her, his black eyes noting the pulses that beat at the base of her creamy throat and at her temples. 'You're acting very foolishly not taking Howard's advice.'

'I don't want anything that's not freely given to me.'

'Then think of it in another way,' he suggested. 'Howard tells me all your mother's money went into setting your father up in business.'

'I expect so.' Laura had never thought of it until then.

'Then you have an entitlement.'

'Do I?'

'We'd better discuss this when you're not dead on your feet,' Blaise told her.

'I don't want to discuss it at all.'

'Then you're a silly little fool.'

'I can't change,' Laura sighed.

He laughed aloud, an unkind sound. 'Don't believe in that. We *all* change, and not always for the better.'

'May I offer you some coffee?' she said, suddenly thinking of the conventions. 'I have very little time.'

'Why?'

She looked up at his face and surprised a vague protectiveness that bewildered her. A hard uncaring she could cope with, but not kindness. She moved fretfully, then gave a small cry as she nearly knocked over an ornament on a side table.

'Steady!' He put out a hand and drew her forward into a chair. 'I'm not going to apologise for my rudeness yesterday, but I am going to offer you a job today.'

'Uncle Howard persuaded you,' stated Laura.

'He thinks you'd benefit by a complete break away. From the look of you this morning, I'm inclined to agree.'

'But it's against your better judgment.'

He smiled sardonically without showing his beautiful white teeth. 'It seems the lesser disaster. In six months you'll feel stronger and your affairs will have begun to be straightened out.'

He had remained standing as he was speaking and instead of feeling menaced by his tall, lean and powerful frame, Laura felt an immediate cessation of strain. It would be so easy to let a strong man make the decisions, but if she went away and left Jamie, her heart would die.

'What are you thinking about?' Blaise asked her, his black eyes grave.

'Uncle Howard told you I have a small brother?'

'And it's tearing your heart out to leave him?'

She looked away from him in some despair. 'What else?'

'We all have to lose someone some time,' he said bitterly.

'Oh, I'm sorry!' She was too afraid to look at him.

'Don't be. I'm not suffering from a broken heart. I no longer have one.'

It did not explain why he was here on an errand of mercy. Jean's rather heavy footsteps were approaching and then she was there, glancing from Laura to their visitor. 'Good morning, sir. Mr Hunter, isn't it?'

'Yes, and you must be Jean.' It was incongruous to see that beautiful smile in the disturbingly sardonic face.

'Surely I can get you some tea . . . coffee?'

'I don't want to disturb you.'

'I'm sure it's not the slightest trouble.' Jean was looking at him steadily but with obvious approval. 'You'll have a cup too, won't you, dear?'

Laura made herself raise her head—such politeness

when she was no longer the daughter of the house and such things were natural. 'Than you, Jean.'

'Do sit down, sir.' Jean urged their visitor warmly, watched him while he did so, then took herself off.

'A positive, kind woman,' Blaise Hunter observed.

'Tremendously kind; more than that, part of the family. The family that *was*.'

'Fight out of it, girl,' he told her. 'You'll have a family of your own.'

'I hope so,' she said, sighing. 'I'm only seeing Jamie's face at the moment. He'll be utterly bewildered when he finds that I'm gone.'

'You mean you haven't said goodbye, or offered some explanation?'

'My stepmother thought it would be wrong of me to try it.' And now her eyes were wet again with tears. 'You can't imagine how terrible it is to have my affairs public!'

'Can't I?' he said very harshly, in his compelling voice. 'Scandals must be made public for the public's enjoyment. The more important one is the more papers it will be in.'

'I've hurt you again,' she sighed.

'No, you haven't,' he snapped. 'You're a nice child. You could even be a very nice child, but don't expect to understand me.' The black eyes were cold and steady. 'No one has come close in years, and the one who did will never be forgiven.'

'No,' she whispered, because he really was intimidating. Virginia, who had been killed trying to flee him. She must have been a reckless person not to have been afraid. Reckless or desperate or both. And yet, strange man that he was, he could show concern.

'What is your little girl's name?' she asked.

'Liza,' he said quietly, 'though really she's a Betsy. I

call her Betsy sometimes. Actually she's a pretty courageous little kid, and you'll know that's not as easy as
it seems. Her mother had the monopoly on looks. Most
people would call Liza a very plain little kid, but in
terms of the human spirit, she's beautiful. For one
thing, she has integrity and she's very loyal. No matter
how many times you feel *you're* against me, don't
mention it to Liza. As far as she's concerned, I'm perfect—a big bear, but perfect.'

'You love her.' Laura smiled gently.

'I admire her a lot.'

'Well then, I will too. Integrity, as I know it, isn't
all that common a quality.'

'Which you will have to face when you do something
about that will. Being noble is one thing; being stupid
is another. You have a fair and just claim, and Howard
is anxious to fight for you.'

'Don't let's talk about it now.' Laura could hear Jean
returning, so she rose to take the tray.

'There we are!' Jean announced in her comfortable
voice. 'While you're having it, I'll continue with the
packing.' The early smile gave way to a look of quiet
sadness and disapproval. 'Perhaps you could tell me,
sir, if you've come to take Laura away?'

'What do you think I *should* do, Jean?' he asked her.

'It's certain, sir, though it breaks my heart to say it,
she *must* go.'

'Then I'll take her when you're ready, but I shall
return this evening to speak to her stepmother. I would
like to have a few moments with the little boy too if I
could. I'm sure if I brought his sister back it would be
chaos, but I think the child is entitled to an explanation
from his sister's new employer. I'll think of some
reason why she left so suddenly and without saying
goodbye.'

Jean, folding her crisp square of apron, gave an exclamation of relief. 'Oh, thank you *so* much, Mr Hunter! His mother will say something to him, I know, but I know you'll think of something better. He'll be bewildered and upset, poor little feller, and I don't know that I can handle it right now. I'm feeling pretty desperate myself.'

'But you're both supposing Paula will consent to seeing Mr Hunter,' Laura cried helplessly. 'However briefly . . . as for *Jamie!*'

Blaise Hunter answered quietly, his voice devoid of expression. 'I'm sure Mrs Mallory will work out that it's in her own best interests.'

He looked magnificent, like a Borgia, and Laura dropped her head into her hands and gave a funny little laugh. 'Let's drink to that,' she said with a terrible gaiety. 'It will be a victory of some sort in among all the torture.'

CHAPTER THREE

In the last half hour, Laura had become increasingly overwhelmed, her awe-filled pleasure edged with a definite feeling of uneasiness. She had often heard and read that the vast Outback was a place of great power, now she was seeing it for the first time in its incredible immensity, and the sight was both breathtaking and oppressive.

It wasn't beautiful country they were flying over, unless beauty lay in immensity, for the limitless plains ran way in a barren flatness, the very emptiness of which had a compelling grandeur. This was the famous

Channel Country where lay the mighty cattle king-
doms, but to Laura's uninitiated eyes it looked like
desert and in every way the most desolate place she
had ever seen.

One couldn't even begin to contemplate being
stranded down there without water or shelter from the
blazing sun. Even beneath the shelter of those queer,
stunted trees the light would be blinding. She had
never experienced such a white-hot radiance in all her
life. The early explorers had died there . . . brave, ill-
fated, ill-prepared men . . . tourists who had yearned
to explore the fabled Inland at first hand and, full of
adventure, had never listened to the warnings of tremendous hazards. Too many journeys started in
triumph, too many deaths . . . thirst, madness, mirage-
filled eyes seared by the imperial sun.

Laura shuddered compulsively and Blaise Hunter
turned on her. 'What's making you so damned nervous?' he demanded with sharp amusement, his fine,
strong hands resting firmly on the control wheel of the
Beech Baron.

'I was just thinking what it might be like stranded
down there.'

'Very difficult.' In his elegant city clothes he had
looked very aloof and formal, now in narrow jeans and
an opened bush shirt that revealed the dark whorls of
hair on his chest he looked far more approachable, but
his sexuality was greatly increased. Laura had not
wanted to notice, but that would have involved not
looking at him at all.

'Have you ever been lost?' she asked him, thinking it
odd how much he disconcerted her.

'Never. Lack of bushcraft can cost you your life.'

'I expect so.'

'What an inadequate little answer! *Know* so—not

that you're going to be allowed to walk off.'

'I felt that.' She stared past the wing at the hard burnt umber land of the mulga. 'It's very daunting, isn't it?' Like you, she wanted to add.

'If you want to put it that way. No sight on earth can give me greater pleasure.' His black eyes flicked over her. 'Love of the land, Miss Mallory. It's a massive obsession, you know. Like the love of money or power, or even women.'

'Naturally they don't have an equal claim,' she said dryly.

'No.' He gave a brief, amused laugh. 'There's a peculiar little imp in you behind those dawn-soft eyes.'

She said nothing but felt a warm flood of heat and colour. In a way, she had been used to admiration all her life, gallantry from older men, eagerness and pleading from her own age group, but she had never felt a quick lurch of desire, and that was what she felt then. It frightened her, for it could not be allowed to happen, and cutting mockery was only his way.

After a few uncomfortable moments she ventured another comment. 'Uncle Howard showed me a picture of Hunter's Moon. I can't imagine it down there.'

'My dear Miss Mallory,' he said, 'an Englishman's home is his castle. What's the point in running a ring around a few thousand square miles if one can't build a fortress-castle? My great-great-grandfather was your typical English gentleman. He only needed money to impose his own life style on the wilds, and he had that.'

'How extraordinary!'

'There were plenty of extraordinary men roaming the Outback—adventurers, explorers, second sons of the British aristocracy, men who saw the chance of founding a dynasty. You should read all the stories about the Honourable Charles Hunter. He was a very dashing gentleman indeed.'

'I'd like that,' she said quite naturally. 'He sounds absolutely fascinating . . . eccentric but sort of a great visionary.'

'That's it exactly,' he said dryly. 'I insist you read the diaries.'

'Why particularly Hunter's Moon?' she asked him.

'One thing and another,' he said absently, beginning to lose altitude. 'The place was a favourite hunting ground for the tribes, Hunter was our name and when you see the house by moonlight you'll understand. Apparently the name presented itself to my illustrious ancestor when he was camped on the original homestead site, pretty well ill and exhausted. As a matter of fact he wrote that he thought he would have died but for the ministrations and potions of the old aboriginal who accompanied him and who remained with him for the rest of his life. A strange friendship, but real. Remember, the old man had never seen a white man before and the stories that reached them wouldn't have been good. As a family we've always treated our black people well and in turn we have their loyalty and in many cases devotion. It's a two-way thing and it works very well.'

'We're dropping,' said Laura, looking down.

'Not dropping, my dear girl—losing altitude, if only for my peace of mind!'

'It must be thrilling to have such a luxurious private airplane,' she commented.

'Hell, all these little-girl words!'

'Didn't you get a thrill when you took possession of it?' she asked him.

'Of course I did,' he smiled at her, and it was like being hit by a giant wave, defeated, engulfed.

She remained sitting quietly while the powerful twin-engined plane homed in over the giant station. It was flooded with brilliant sunlight and she saw the maze of channels and waterways that in the good seasons filled up with life-giving water; the great natural irrigation system that slumbered until the skies darkened and rivulets turned into an inland sea. In the distance, a line of flat-topped mesas, indigo in colour, over which the silver-blue mirage leapt like a flame. Directly beneath, the looping, glittering line of a creek, belted by trees, green trees with glossy foliage, thicker on one side, and now she could see the shining waters were festooned with blue flowers . . . waterlilies, hundreds of them.

'How beautiful!' she burst out involuntarily.

A group of men on horses, surrounding cattle in a holding yard, looked up to wave, a tribute to the homecoming Hunter, while further in it looked more like an oasis, the harsh land giving way to a curiously cultivated settlement for all the world like a small town in a Western movie. There were buildings at regular intervals, large buildings, small buildings, neat white bungalows. Outside one of them two small children were waving happily. But none of this seemed important.

Dominating the landscape with its sheer beauty was a Colonial variation of an imposing Georgian mansion, outstanding anywhere, but mind-boggling set down in this immensely isolated, incredibly bizarre canvas. One could refuse at first to believe it. It was like finding a masterpiece worlds removed from its original site, and its very unexpectedness reduced Laura to silence. Whatever happened to her at Hunter's Moon *had* to be extraordinary. The whole place was heroic.

*

The room into which Mrs Madden, the housekeeper, led her was at least twice the size of her old bedroom at home, but despite its volume comfortable and romantic in the extreme. No governess's little cubicle, this, but the beautiful bedroom of a young lady, with a mahogany four-poster bed, a carved mantel, gleaming polished floor and an antique Persian rug, two matching armchairs on either side of a small circular table, a tall cabinet and a low brassbound chest, there was even a plump ottoman with tassels and someone had made the very charming and welcoming gesture of filling a Chinese blue and white vase with flowers.

'I hadn't expected this,' said Laura in a soft voice.

'Mr Hunter thought it would suit you,' the housekeeper told her unexpectedly. 'Liza picked the flowers especially and arranged them herself.'

'Really?' Laura found her eyes shimmering. 'How nice!'

'I expect you're tired, dear?' Mrs Madden, a homely but efficient-looking body, was looking Laura over thoroughly but pleasantly. 'It's a long trip.'

'Yes, it is, but I found it extraordinarily rewarding. I've never visited the Outback before.'

'It's the best place on earth!' Mrs Madden maintained, apparently finding nothing extraordinary in Laura's wishing to bury herself in the wilds. 'Now if there's anything I can help you with, just let me know. We're all very pleased you've arrived. Liza is very excited.'

'Where is she?' Laura met those kind blue eyes.

'Miss Judith took her out. That is, Mrs Steven Hunter. You'll meet all the family at dinner, but right now I suggest you take a nap. You look a mite pale.'

'That's because you've all got a tan,' Laura smiled.

'Skin like an old camel, that's what *I've* got,' Mrs

Madden returned the smile. 'Mustn't ever forget to wear your hat when you're in the sun, love, or you'll soon lose that beautiful peaches and cream. A right lovely young lady, aren't you?'

'It's kind of you to say so,' Laura looked away rather shyly. 'Shall I be dining with the family, Mrs Madden?'

'Now where else would you be?' the blue eyes sparkled goodnaturedly. 'The child doesn't, of course. The family dine too late in any case and young Liza is up with the birds.' While she was speaking, Mrs Madden walked to a side door and opened it up. 'You and Liza can make this into your own private little sitting room. Her bedroom is on the other side. You'll be sharing the bathroom, as I've shown you, but in this wing of the house you'll be very private. Mr Hunter has his parents' old suite in the east wing near his grandmother and Mr and Mrs Steven Hunter like the big bedroom off the top of the stairs.'

Laura lifted her blonde head and spoke seriously. 'It's such a very large house I expect I shall lose myself.'

'Didn't I when I first came here twenty odd years ago? Never mind, my dear, you'll soon get used to it. I expect Mr Hunter will show you around the house when he has time. He cares a great deal about it, though it costs a fortune to maintain.'

Laura was so tired, and feeling so far removed from reality, she drifted off as soon as her head touched the pillow. Such a delicious fragrance! She didn't know it was the native boronia. Everything of her old life had been taken from her, and though she wanted to cry out to the heavens for help she knew she had to get through on her own. Liza wouldn't realise how much her sweet little gesture had impressed her. Physical beauty was

something, like porcelain, but a tender heart was much
better. Even Blaise Hunter wasn't as heartless as he
claimed, for he had done something very wonderful
for her in confronting Paula and getting through to
speak to Jamie. Jamie, however much he missed her,
would think she was on some wonderful mission, and
she had arranged for Jean to collect her letters and
read them to Jamie at bedtime. Paula would hate it,
but she couldn't send Jean away. Jean was too good at
her job and devoted to Jamie.

Jamie.

When she woke up trembling and bewildered a small
round face was staring at her.

'You've been crying.'

'Have I?' Laura touched her cheek with her left hand.

'See, there are the tears,' the child said simply.

'I must have been dreaming,' Laura remarked, sitting up and swinging her feet to the floor.

'It must have been a sad dream,' the little girl said
encouragingly.

'It was, Liza,' Laura smiled, and took the little girl's
hand. 'But I don't feel sad now. I have a friend. Thank
you for putting the flowers in my room. They said
welcome.'

'You like them?' The little girl clasped Laura's hand
tightly.

'They made me feel glad.'

Liza smiled, the wavering smile growing stronger.
'Claudia thought that was going too far.'

'And who's Claudia?' Laura asked.

'Aunty Judith's sister.' Liza's small, stocky body
seemed to crumple. 'I don't think she likes me.'

'Why not?' Laura's tone of voice implied, who
wouldn't?

'She's always telling me to go away. Once when I

opened the door of Aunty Judith's room I heard Claudia telling her I was hopeless.'

'At what?'

Liza neither moved nor spoke for a moment. 'I don't know. I expect it's because I don't like horses.'

Laura could well see this might create a problem. 'But they're such beautiful creatures, don't you think?'

'Too big!' Liza complained, obviously with the memory of some painful experience. 'Claudia can ride like the wind.'

'Because,' Laura explained, 'she's had lots of practice.'

'So has Aunty Judith, but she can't ride as well.'

'I expect it's a case of one liking riding more than the other. I'm sure there are plenty of things you can do.'

'Nothing!' said Liza, with a long frustrated sigh. 'That's why Blaise has sent for you.'

'You call your father Blaise?' Laura asked softly, very much surprised.

'Yes.' Round, bright blue eyes looked into hers enquiringly. 'Blaise lets me do whatever I like. That is, if it's absolutely safe. I'm not allowed to swim in the pool or the creek by myself.'

'You're not a strong swimmer?' Laura was studying the little girl gently. Plain of feature she might have been, but there was something very pleasing about her, a direct gaze and a likeable personality.

'I'm sure *you* are.' The little girl was looking at Laura admiringly.

'And I'll be pleased to help you. My work here is primarily for your lessons, but there are lots of other things I might be able to help you with as well. When you care to try it, I'll probably be able to help you ride a horse.'

'That's very kind of you,' Liza said nervously.

'We won't try it until you're ready. Perhaps you had a bad experience, but if we do it the right way, I'm sure you won't again.'

'Haven't you got the most beautiful hair?' Liza commented. 'Mine is such a terrible bother.'

'Why don't you get it cut?' Laura looked at the child's beige-coloured hair that hung limply past her shoulders.

'It's too thin.' Liza grabbed clumsily at a swathe.

'Then we'll tie it back with a ribbon.'

'I'm not the ribbon type.' Liza turned and looked at herself in the long mirror. 'One way and another I need a lot of help.'

Laura didn't press her. 'Goodness,' she exclaimed, glancing at the clock, 'look at the time!'

'Annie thought it was better to let you sleep,' Liza explained.

'Who's Annie?'

'Mrs Madden,' Liza answered. 'Claudia is the only one who calls her Mrs Madden. We all call her Annie. It's easier.'

'And you must call me Laura.'

'It's a lovely name,' Liza glanced at Laura's hair again, 'and it suits you. Did you know Blaise calls me Betsy?'

'He did mention it.'

'I'm the Boss's daughter.'

'And I like you and I want you to like me.'

'Oh, *yes*!' Liza twined her fingers together. 'I think I should warn you I'm not smart. My last governess called me a very nice little girl but not a serious student.'

'You've had another governess, then?' Laura moved

across the room to switch on the main light.

'Oh yes,' Liza told her sweetly. 'I've had two, but they both fell in love with Blaise. Claudia said you will too, count on it.'

'My only answer to that, Liza,' Laura looked back at the child, 'is one can't very well count on anything in this world.'

'I *know*. For instance, Claudia told Aunty Judith you'd probably be just another silly little idiot, but I'll bet she'd love to look like you. Annie said just looking at you was a pleasure.'

It was obvious that Liza, living alone with adults, was listening in to far too many conversations, and she gathered her compact little body to tell Laura more, but Laura forestalled her. 'I expect I'll have to decide what I'm wearing tonight.'

Liza smiled again in real pleasure. 'All right. I'll help you. Claudia has so many clothes, it's incredible!'

They chatted very happily, as a matter of habit, as if they had known one another for years. 'If anything's not right you can fix it any way you like,' Liza told her, spraying herself faintly with some of Laura's Caline. 'That's nice, isn't it?' She dipped her little snub nose into the crook of her elbow, savouring the scent. 'I don't like Claudia's perfume. It's too strong.'

'Is Claudia staying long?' Laura couldn't resist asking.

'She's only just arrived.' Liza gave her a glance that was almost adult. 'She didn't really need to come again, but I expect she wanted to see you.' The child brightened, walked up to Laura and held her hand. 'Anyway, I don't care what Claudia says, somebody has to take care of me, and I want it to be *you*.'

'We'll shake on that,' Laura commented with a smile, but the little girl gazed back at her seriously.

'It's very nice to know you, Laura, and I hope you like it out here very much.' It was said with such intensity Laura was certain Liza was expressing deep, hidden feelings. So small, so young to lose her mother. On a wave of compassion Laura hugged the little girl to her side and as they both looked up at a tap on the open door, Blaise Hunter was looking at them.

'I see you've met,' he remarked.

Liza's plain little face lit up like magic. 'Welcome *home*!' She made a rush at that tall, lithe figure and he lifted her like a leaf.

'Hi, Betsy!'

'Hi, Blaise.'

Whatever his feelings for the female of the species he certainly tempered them for his child. So he could hate and he could love. He could condemn and make an exception. He was certainly a man of strong emotion no matter how tightly controlled.

Carefully he set the child on her feet and glanced up at Laura, watching them so intently with her luminous eyes.

'Everything suit you?'

'Very much.' She looked quickly around the beautiful big room. 'I didn't expect so much grandeur.'

'We're out to make you happy.'

'That's *right*!' Liza seconded happily, with a protective, maternal note. 'Laura was crying when I woke her up.'

'Just a dream,' Laura remarked quickly.

'It was sad,' Liza told her father, nodding her head emphatically. 'I suppose Laura was missing her family.'

'That's right,' he told her, and gave Laura a sharp, penetrating glance. 'Now that you've met Liza, I'll take her off. We have dinner at seven o'clock, but come down before that and meet the family.'

'And wear that green dress,' Liza told her, then smiled up at her father. 'We picked it out, just the two of us!'

Just over an hour later Laura made her way down the impressive divided staircase wearing the almond green dress Liza had liked so much. A sound of laughter came from the great drawing room and she moved towards that particularly brilliant and brittle peal, guessing before she even entered the room that it would be the outspoken Claudia.

'Ah, there you are, Miss Mallory,' Blaise Hunter turned his sleek raven head as Laura entered the room. 'Come in and meet the family.'

They were all staring up at her with varying degrees of surprise, and a tall, slim man who looked a shadow version of his brother rose to his feet, the rather blank expression on his face giving way to a charming smile.

Two very striking-looking women were sitting on a sofa upholstered in embroidered silk, and a little distance away an old lady with beautifully dressed pure white hair was sitting up regally in a tall chair like a throne.

It was she who spoke first and held out a hand Laura quickly saw was knotted with arthritis. 'Welcome to Hunter's Moon, my dear,' she said with such warmth Laura smiled at her in gratitude.

'Thank you, Mrs Hunter.' The dark eyes that once must have been as black and brilliant as her grandson's were studying her comprehensively but certainly not offensively—which was more than Laura could say of the other two women.

They were very much alike, like two scarlet poppies—dark-haired, dark-eyed with strong, prominent bone structure, clear, golden skins and full-lipped lush mouths. One appeared to soften, Judith Hunter, as Blaise made the introductions, but the younger sister, Claudia, jerked her head back in near effrontery. 'How d'you do,' she murmured with a conspicuous lack of warmth.

Even Mr Steven Hunter's eyes had opened wide; not jet-black like his brother's, but a gold-flecked light brown. 'Tell me,' he asked in a light, amused tone, 'what a girl like you would be doing as a governess?'

'Yes, *do* tell us.' Claudia's voice asked from behind him, malice lending its flatness a little colour.

'I needed a job,' Laura said simply.

'But to retire to a remote cattle station?' Claudia persisted, narrowing her long eyes.

'What I've seen has fascinated me.' Laura moved to the chair the old Mrs Hunter's frail hand indicated—mercifully, beside her. 'I know I'm going to enjoy my stay here, and Liza is a very nice little girl.'

'You've met her?' Claudia snapped.

'Certainly,' Laura smiled, not knowing that in the heavy ornately carved Victorian armchair she looked like a priceless piece of porcelain. 'Very happily too. We made friends at once.'

'Good for you!' the old lady laughed spontaneously. 'Now, a sherry for Laura, I think. I'm not going to call you Miss Mallory, my dear. It was all very correct in my day, but mercifully that day is past.'

'What kind of work *have* you been doing?' Claudia clipped in.

'The interview is over, Claudia,' Blaise Hunter remarked dryly. 'Laura is a university student with a year left to go.'

· '*What?*'

'Better tell us, Laura,' Steven Hunter smiled at her, 'so we can all understand.'

'It's not a pretty thing to be nosey,' his grandmother remarked. 'Laura is what she appears to be, a well bred, well educated young lady, and that's what we want.'

'No questions,' Steven Hunter laughed, and tossed his drink down. It wasn't sherry, Laura noted, but the colour of good whisky. It would be hard, she thought, to be a watered down version of one's older brother, but she supposed he was used to it. The first place, the place of honour, was only reserved for one.

Dinner, she was to discover, was superb, but Claudia directed so many questions at her, innocent for the most part but laced with challenge and a distinctly patronising tone, Laura couldn't do justice to it. Claudia wasn't embarrassing her, Laura had too much natural poise, but she was dampening what little enthusiasm she had for a new life.

After dinner old Mrs Hunter retired early, speaking pleasantly to Laura for two minutes and promising that they would have a long talk in the morning. She had, as Laura found out later, made a special effort to come down to dinner for Laura's sake, although she had been in considerable pain for most of the day.

'Come, Miss Mallory,' Blaise ordered her, 'and I'll show you around the house, I may not find the time again.'

'But surely I can do that tomorrow?' Claudia looked up at him in dismay.

'Better now,' Blaise returned convincingly. 'It's a very large house, as you can see, Miss Mallory,' he began to explain, 'but a lot of the rooms are locked up.'

They began with the formal dining room, the room the family called the Gold Room because of the magnificent gold wallpaper, and worked their way through the ground floor, excluding the kitchen wing which was Mrs Madden's exclusive domain—and small wonder, Laura thought. The woman was a genius, not merely a first-class cook.

'When the Honourable Charles Hunter built this house,' Blaise told her, 'he was wealthy, but over the years he became very rich indeed. Of course a lot of people thought him quite mad, including his family in England, but genius and madness, as we all know, exist at the same time. From a privileged and pampered young man he became one of the great pioneers. The British have always fulfilled their roles admirably. Paradoxical people, really, exceptionally sophisticated, yet haring off to the wilds. By the time he died aged eighty-nine, he called Australia his home.'

'Is that a portrait of him in the gallery?' Laura asked, passing under one of the series of gothic arches.

'No,' Blaise Hunter paused and opened, a door, 'the only portrait we have of him is here in my study.' He stood back so she could precede him into the room, a much smaller room than the huge library and in no way as grandiose. The ceiling was richly decorated, as were all the ceilings right through the house, but Blaise Hunter's study was furnished in the manner of a man who had considerable work to get through. It was comfortable, functional, wood-panelled, and over the mantel was a portrait of a seated gentleman with an open book on one knee.

'How handsome!' Laura took pleasure in going forward and staring up. 'He's even a lot like you.'

'Does this mean you find me handsome?'

'I prefer him.'

'I needed that.' He laughed briefly but the sound of it remained.

'No wonder you love this house,' she said sincerely. 'I suppose you'd do anything to keep it?'

'I used to think I would,' he said harshly, 'but now I'm not so sure. Particularly as I have no son.'

'But surely you'll remarry?' *Claudia*, she thought.

'You'd advise it?' He looked down his autocratic, straight nose at her, defying her to extol the virtues of marriage.

'If you want a son.' She remained motionless, staring up at him, her ash-blonde head on line with his shoulder.

'I'm afraid I have nothing to offer a woman, and women are very demanding.'

'You mean they need constant affection?'

'I mean they bore me.'

'In that case I'll keep out of your way,' she said dryly.

'You can in a day or two,' he said, suddenly smiling lazily; a sight that still shocked her and made her look away. 'I don't think you need to wear green silk again after tonight. No doubt you consider it your best colour.'

'Sorry to disappoint you, Mr Hunter,' she picked up a glass paperweight and put it down again, 'white looks well on me, so does a certain shade of red. Liza picked my dress out, you might remember.'

'Obviously she's taken to you,' he commented.

'Don't sound as if that's not what you want!'

They were, she realised, almost quarrelling, just as she realised it was a man–woman confrontation and not employer–employee.

'Good God,' he said dryly, 'am I as obvious as all that?'

'Please,' she said in a soft, placating voice, 'I didn't intend to be rude, but you know you're trying to provoke me.'

'Something, I profess, I like.'

'Why?' she raised her head.

'Why?' He only repeated the word after her, a bitter twist to his shapely mouth. 'Come along, Miss Mallory. We've seen all we need to see here. Now the next floor.'

From the gallery they could look down at the lofty entrance hall with its elaborately carved oak woodwork, opulent chandelier and the polychromed parquet floor, and as they began to walk along Blaise Hunter switched on a few lights. Portraits sprang to life, a valuable collection of early Australian art, major paintings such as Laura had seen in State Art Galleries ... Glover, Martens, Buvelot, Von Guerard, a very grand painting by the Swiss Nicholas Chavalier and a number by William Strutt.

'The Impressionist painters are downstairs,' he told her.

'I noticed.' Indeed she had, for she was a great art lover and quite talented with a pencil or crayon, although she had never taken herself seriously.

They began to talk about art and she found him immensely knowledgeable, and their common interest acted as a balance for the kind of sexual hostility that seemed to flare between them unexpectedly.

She lost count of the number of bedrooms. It would have made a splendid grand hotel, but they didn't hurry as though they had a lot of time on their hands.

'Who does all the dusting?' she asked. She had thought her own home large in scale, as it was compared to the average suburban house, but this really was a mansion where the ghosts could roam around all night.

'I'm terribly sorry, you may be required to do that.'

'I have very limited domestic skills,' she assured him.

'And I was looking for an asset!' He clicked his tongue.

'Actually you haven't outlined my duties,' Laura reminded him.

'Haven't I?' He was back to being hard and provoking. 'Fate put you into this role, not me.'

'You admit it?'

His voice was quite matter-of-fact. 'You know damned well I didn't want you here, but since you are we must get on with it. Liza, I've been told, is a little below average with her studies. I'm sure with just a little extra work you can bring her up to scratch. It's the *way* information is presented that counts. I have a feeling you'll make her a good teacher, and with children I'm sure you're very gentle and patient. You don't have to work yourself or Liza silly. Set yourself a daily target and when it's done you're both free to do as you like. Only a few things I ask—don't attempt to tantalise my men. I'd greatly appreciate it if you'd be friendly but aloof.'

'Is that possible?' she asked wonderingly.

'You know exactly what I mean.' The frail link of well-being snapped between them. 'You're a beautiful girl, and they don't fit in well.'

'That's rubbish!' she snapped, for just a moment feeling furious.

'Fancy that,' he said smoothly. 'I didn't think shadowed eyes flashed.'

She couldn't return that cool, sleek stare. 'What else don't you want me to do?'

'The unexpected,' he said sarcastically, though his expression said he meant to be obeyed. 'Don't go wandering off on your own, or take Liza in tow. It's important you keep within a couple of miles of the compound. I never asked you, but I certainly hope you ride?'

'As a matter of fact I can only just stay on.' It wasn't the truth either.

'The right mount and a little practice and you'll improve.' His black eyes pinned her to the wall. 'Liza hasn't the slightest interest in horses. In fact, she's frightened of them.'

'Then I shall tell her stories.'

'How delightful!' he turned away. 'Though I should prefer it if you could teach her how to ride. I've tried, Claudia has tried, we've *all* tried, but Liza is so pent up with fear she makes my heart ache.'

'Which proves you really do have a heart.' Laura allowed herself to smile at him, but instead of responding the handsome features tautened, intensely male and curiously alert.

'Which won't, Miss Mallory, make any difference to *you*.'

They stood silently before each other and for a moment she felt as though her body had no weight and she was being held upright by his gaze. There were so many things to be aware of, his height and male splendour, her fragile defence. 'You never let me finish about those stories,' she almost whispered, and when he made an abrupt movement away from her, she caught at his sleeve.

'Wait! Please let me finish. Why have I made you angry? I'll tell Liza all about the horse's place in history, in art. I'll tell her about the Paleolithic cave drawings in France, the way Chinese legend extolled that proud and noble creature, Greek mythology, about that great white winged creature Pegasus, the way Apollo, the sun god, drove his fiery horses across the sky; the way he still does at sunset. I'll find pictures of pottery and bronzes. I'll get her interested, then I'll teach her to ride.'

'You might too.' He looked down at her small hand tightly gripping his arm. 'You are constantly surprising me, Miss Mallory. What do you want to say now?'

'Why, nothing.' She took her hand away. 'That's all.'

'What a pity, when you were just showing yourself a lively fighter. Now, there's nothing to interest you from here on. Up those stairs is only used for storage. Anyway, I don't have the keys.'

'Thank you. I should be able to find my way around much better.'

They walked slowly back downstairs, but not a hint of companionability remained. Laura knew that he had objected to her grasping his arm, she had felt the dark hostility in him, the tightening of muscle. A woman's touch, the brand of shame. Certainly he had not forgotten his brief, unhappy marriage, as though no woman could offer constancy and beauty was her only garment.

Claudia, her tall, pencil-slim body stretched into a straight line, was waiting for them at the bottom of the great stairway. She probably didn't know it, but she wasn't controlling her anger very well. Though her face was lacquered over, expressionless, her dark eyes displayed her true feelings.

'You've been rather a long time,' she gave them both a tight smile.

'Did you get tired of waiting?' Blaise smiled at her with sleek urbanity.

'Yes, I was coming after you.' She stalked towards him, elemental, feline, but hiding her outrage. 'You realise I haven't seen you for *six* weeks, and I've so much to tell you.'

'You'll excuse me, won't you?' Laura said politely. 'It's been rather a tiring day.'

Claudia smiled contemptuously. 'If you tire easily, Miss Mallory, you don't belong here.'

'Oh, I'm strong enough in my own quiet sort of way.' Laura glanced away from Claudia to Blaise Hunter's tall, elegant figure. 'Goodnight, Mr Hunter.'

'Miss Mallory.' He bowed slightly with hard, mocking charm. 'The household usually have breakfast any time between six and eight. Most likely I'll be able to show you around the compound some time after that.'

'But, Blaise, you'll be neglecting your work!' Claudia exclaimed with finality, her faintly grating voice coldly metallic.

He looked at her and shrugged, disclaiming such a preposterous statement. 'I thought you said once I worked far too hard?'

'I. . . .' Claudia sighed and incredibly raised one hand to his cheek. 'You're impossible, Blaise!'

Laura didn't want to listen to any more. A blind man could have learned everything from Claudia's tone alone. Laura, with her perfect eyesight, saw a woman who was hopelessly in love, a woman who wanted this man in the most primitive way possible.

'Oh!' she cried aloud as she flopped limply on her bed. It was a betrayal of anxiety, for her own emotions were suddenly naked to her. Much as she deplored it and was prepared to fight the force of it, she was intensely attracted to Blaise Hunter herself. In her mind's eyes she saw his brilliant eyes and the shape of his mouth. She was thinking what it might be like to be made love to by a man like that. Of being—— With a groan she swung over and hid her burning face in the lace-frothed pillow.

CHAPTER FOUR

BREAKFAST was in the traditional English fashion, lavish, but Laura was a small eater at that time of the day.

'Now, now, miss, you need your protein,' Mrs Madden protested, sounding very much like Jean. 'Won't you have an egg or some bacon?'

'No, honestly, not this morning, I couldn't.' Laura softened her refusal with a smile. 'That was a superb dinner last night.'

'You must tell me the sort of dishes you like,' Mrs Madden suggested. 'I hope you're going to have some toast and marmalade?'

'Actually I never eat marmalade at all.'

'Good gracious!' Mrs Madden responded, somewhat nonplussed. 'I thought everyone liked marmalade.'

Liza burst in on them wreathed in smiles. 'Good morning, Annie,' Mrs Madden patted her cosily. '' Morning, Laura.'

'Good morning.' Laura thrust back a chair and Liza slipped into it.

'I'm the one who's usually up early, but I slept in.'

Behind them Mrs Madden was busy chinking dishes. 'Here you are, young lady.' She set a dish of sliced peaches in front of the child. 'When you finish that you can have your muesli.'

'Oh, really, do I have to have it this morning?' Liza complained.

'Yes, you have, so don't complain.'

'I think it's perfectly absurd the way everyone has to

have cereal,' Liza muttered, then decided to smile again. 'I've been trying to decide all the things we should do today. It's so difficult—I'm a ditherer.'

'Your father told me he might show me around the compound,' Laura told her, deciding there wasn't the slightest trace of Blaise Hunter in his sturdy little daughter. It was perfectly clear she took after somebody in her mother's family.

'Oh, great!' Liza flushed with pleasure and even accepted her muesli with a smile. 'He's being nicer to you than Miss Grierson.'

'Your last governess?'

'And a very impressionable young lady,' Mrs Madden suddenly guffawed. 'If you girls can help yourselves I'll make fresh tea for the others. Miss Judith isn't up yet and neither is her sister.'

'Thank goodness!' said Liza, and gave a faintly hysterical giggle. 'I think I might have a sausage now.'

'I'll get it,' Laura offered.

There was so much left on the sideboard, Laura was befuddled. The ladies of the house had to be extravagant eaters, yet that didn't seem likely, with their pencil-slim figures.

She had scarcely sat down again before Mrs Steven Hunter appeared, yawning delicately behind her hand.

'Well met this morning?' she asked politely.

'Fine, thank you.'

'Oh, I didn't sleep at all,' Liza announced with some triumph. 'I was so excited.'

'Really, dear? Why?'

'Why, Laura's here, of course,' Liza replied, undeterred.

'May her star never set!' Judith said ironically, peering under the silver lids on the sideboard. 'No devilled kidneys with the bacon?' she queried aggrievedly.

It had to be the only thing that wasn't there.

Judith sat down again with her breakfast compote, tasted it gingerly, as though it might be laced with poison, then proceeded to spoon in. 'What's on the agenda today?' she asked languidly, then made a lightning change to sharpness. 'Really, Liza, that's no way to cut your sausage. You're quite a big enough girl to handle a knife and fork properly.'

'Oh, drat it!' Startled, Liza ventured a more aggressive stab and the crisp pork sausage suddenly shot off her plate and landed inertly on the dark golden polished floor.

Judith sighed and stared up at the ceiling.

'It's just that it's so *fat*!' Liza said apologetically. 'Frankly I don't feel like it any more.' She darted up, jostled her cereal bowl so it teetered on the edge and grasped the offending sausage with her napkin. 'I'll take this through to the kitchen,' she said.

'Naturally!' Judith sighed again.

She was, Laura decided, rather a pain in the neck, and in the morning light not quite as striking as she had appeared the night before.

'Accidents will happen,' Laura murmured comfortingly.

'They happen a good deal around Liza,' Judith told her coolly. 'But you have yet to find that out.'

Not surprisingly Liza didn't return, though she had been tucking in quite happily, but before Laura could make her getaway, Claudia made her entrance, clearly the dominant sister and a very businesslike figure in immaculately cut riding clothes.

'Good morning,' she said shortly, though she favoured her sister with a slight smile.

Laura murmured politely and went to rise.

'Oh, do sit down again, Miss Mallory,' Claudia

ordered her. 'There's so much about you we'd like to know.' Claudia walked over to the sideboard, and Laura was amazed to see her slip. 'What's that grease!' Claudia screeched.

'Liza dropped something,' her sister told her, undistracted from her scrambled eggs with mushrooms.

'How disgusting!' Robbed of her superb equilibrium, Claudia was now in a foul temper. 'Call Mrs Madden and have her clean it up.'

'Call her yourself,' Judith suggested with amazing indifference.

For a moment Laura thought she would collapse with laughter, but Claudia's furiously embarrassed eyes were on her. 'Would you mind going through to the kitchen and asking Mrs Madden to clean up this mess. After all, you work here.'

'Why, certainly.' That suited Laura exactly, so she too made her escape. Had she stayed heaven knows what their exchange might have resulted in. The most amazing aspect of the whole thing was the two sisters' attitude towards Liza, the only child of a powerful and high-mettled man. One might have expected them both to strain themselves to the limit trying to be pleasant, yet they scarcely bothered to hide their impatient intolerance. There was no excuse for Claudia, and even less for Judith, Liza's aunt by marriage. It was most strange.

Mrs Madden's domain would have been fallen on gleefully by Robert Carrier or any other really famous cook. It had everything necessary for the perfect preparation and cooking of dishes for every possible occasion and for large numbers but combined with the sheer professionalism was the feeling of some wonderful old farmhouse. Laura loved it at once.

So too, apparently did Liza, because she was seated at an ample breakfast nook making repeated scoops into a large glass of milk topped with far to much Milo. Mrs Madden had her back to her at the sculptured sinks, painstakingly impressing on two little Aboriginal housegirls the need for an absolutely sparkling wash-up. A dishwasher there might have been, but no dish-washer ever built could possibly cope with the vast pile-up of the station's breakfast dishes, pots and pans.

'Mrs Madden!' Laura called, to make herself heard.

'Who's that?' Mrs Madden demanded, the frown on her face straightening out as soon as she saw it was Laura. 'Are you looking for Liza, dear?' she asked.

'Hi!' Liza looked up to give Laura a Milo-moustached smile, while the round chocolate faces of the little housegirls registered smiles and lots of dimples.

'I'm afraid there's a little bit of grease on the dining-room floor,' Laura explained herself. 'If you'll give me a dishcloth I'll wipe it up.'

'That would be my sausage,' Liza murmured unhappily.

'Gracious!' Mrs Madden caught up a sponge. 'A spot of detergent should fix it. You take Liza off, my dear.' Mrs Madden nodded towards the back door with the quick look of a woman who was used to storms. 'By the way, I'd like you to meet Marilyn and Kate, two of my brood. They've only begun their training.'

'How are you, girls?' Laura enquired smilingly, and was rewarded by those enchanting shy grins.

'If Blaise takes the jeep there'll be plenty of room for me.' Liza hopped up from her seat and flashed to Laura's side, pausing to give a sharp cry of pain as she struck her knee on the half opened door of a cupboard.

'I keep telling you, Liza, to slow down,' Mrs

Madden cautioned, and smiled approvingly as Laura took the child's hand.

It was nearly mid-morning before Blaise returned for them, but Laura and Liza had all but locked themselves in the schoolroom in an unspoken effort to spare themselves social contact. Blaise found them there, Liza going back and forth in an old family rocking chair, while Laura was seated at the long table going through Liza's old exercise books, seeing plainly that she would have a lot of work ahead.

Her expression as she looked down was engrossed, so it took Liza's delighted little cry to make her glance up. 'Oh, good morning, Mr Hunter.'

'Miss Mallory,' he seemed to stress it, the mockery and his black eyes bedevilling her to the skin.

'I can come with you, can't I, Blaise? *Please!*' begged Liza.

'Sure you can,' he said briskly, 'but we have to go now. I'm having the vet flying in this afternoon, so I'll be busy then.'

Laura closed the books quickly and stood up, feeling the most peculiar throbbing in her veins. Blaise Hunter was examining her from head to toe and quite simply she didn't know how to handle it.

'Your arms will get burnt,' he said finally. She was wearing yellow jeans and a white ribbed T-shirt like a singlet.

'Actually I tan quite easily,' she told him.

'You might where you come from. Here, you'll burn.'

'If you say so,' she said politely.

'We'll have to find Laura a hat with a wide brim,' Liza told him in her quaint, motherly fashion.

'Damn, haven't you got one?' He looked very hard, very masculine and impatient.

'I left in a hurry, remember?' she said quickly, and now the wild, salty tears were in her throat. What was Jamie doing this morning? Dear little girl that Liza was, she was no substitute for a beloved little brother.

Extraordinarily he jerked her chin up. 'Don't you dare cry.'

'You're crazy!'

Liza looked at them breathlessly. Whoever called *Blaise* crazy?

His far-seeing brilliant eyes were still on Laura's flushed face and shimmering eyes. 'That housekeeper of yours is a very capable woman,' he reminded her.

'I know.' It was the oddest sensation she had ever known, his hand on her skin.

'Shall I get Laura a hat from the shop?' Liza asked, mystified.

'Thanks, pet.' Blaise Hunter flashed her an approving glance. 'You're a smart little kid in all the practical ways that count.'

He too spoke to Liza in a curious fashion. Not the language of a loving father, more an affectionate uncle. Hadn't Laura's own father called her 'my little princess'? Far-off days, the halcyon days before Paula.

The slouch hat Liza found her was the smallest the station stocked and Laura had to use the fullness of her hair to pad it out. It was a hasty job and needless to say ash-blonde strands escaped, not untidily as she feared, but rather charmingly. At least Liza thought so, ever vigilant on Laura's behalf. Those tears at their first meeting had done it, for Liza was nothing if not tenderhearted. She couldn't, for instance, bear to see the calves branded, a brumby broken, a dingo shot or a baby kangaroo that looked as if it had lost its mother.

They were all nicely settled in the jeep when Claudia cried imperiously from the portico with its tall white

Corinthian columns, 'I say, you're not going without me, surely?'

'*Can't* we, Blaise?' Liza muttered sotto voce.

'Shall I get in the back?' Laura was already organising herself to do so. As an eligible bride for the master of Hunter's Moon Claudia was entitled to the front seat.

Now she sprinted down to the jeep, a most impressive sight in her riding clothes and a very expensive-looking lady's version of Blaise Hunter's stetson.

'You should have stayed in the front seat, Laura,' Liza hissed indignantly. 'I'd sooner have a bad time myself.'

'Please be quiet,' Blaise warned laconically.

'For pity's sake, Blaise,' Claudia announced a shade sharply, 'there was absolutely no need for you to bother about this. I could have taken Miss Mallory on a tour.' Poor helpless creature! her tone added.

'Maybe I feel like the ride,' he answered with a sort of amusement. 'I thought we'd run out as far as Eight Mile Swamp and work our way in.'

'Wouldn't it have been more pleasant to take the horses?' Claudia couldn't seem to take her eyes off his profile.

'Then we wouldn't have been able to take Betsy and perhaps Miss Mallory. From what she tells me she needs a lot more practice.'

'You *can* ride?' Claudia deigned to turn her crisply curling head, whorls fitting neatly to her nape.

'Yes,' Laura answered shortly. Why tell her I'm damned good? she thought. Her father had bought her her first pony almost before she could walk and she had belonged to an excellent club. But no one but herself and maybe Liza needed to know that for a while.

They ran past the offices, the store, the saddle sheds,

the large building for machinery, delightful-looking white cottages surrounded by the brilliant, bright colours of tropical shrubs and vines; past more solid-looking buildings, the giant hangar where the Beech Baron and the station helicopter were housed, beyond the perimeter of the station compound to the plain country that ran out as far as the eye could see.

The sun was up full power and Laura was glad now of the checked shirt she had pulled on like a jacket. They flew over a bump and Liza yelled happily, 'Yippee!' her round little face with its smattering of freckles engaging in its love of life. It taught Laura a lesson. Liza had suffered the loss of her mother, but she had learned to look on life again and love it. They sat close together, hand in hand, Laura trying to absorb everything she was seeing.

'Stallion Creek,' Liza told her. 'We're not allowed to swim there. That's where the horses cross.'

There were birds in their millions, a common sight for the rest of them, but Laura had never seen anything like it in her life. Budgerigars followed them in a dense green cloud, white corellas and pink and grey galahs packed the trees along with parrots, their brilliant plumage necked with yellow, and high up, above the predatory hawks and the falcons, a solitary eagle, its great wings outstretched as it rode a thermal mat.

'When the rivers come down in flood,' Liza confided, 'all the water birds flock in to breed. Hunter's Moon is a major breeding ground for no-madic birds. The lignum swamps are full of them like a holiday camp—colonies of ibis. Blaise is pretty happy to see them because they eat all the grasshoppers and caterpillars that strip the grasses and herbage.'

'You're very knowledgeable, Liza,' Laura smiled.

'Yes, I am,' Liza agreed. 'But I've never been able

to get to where the pelican colonies breed. They like the remote swamps. I've seen them flying, of course, but I'd sure like to know where they build their nests.'

On the mirage-blurred horizon low hills rose from the plain and beyond the hills the immeasurable miles of sand and the Wild Heart. Here the dunes, a deep red colour, were sculptured by the shifting winds, rising to pyramids of a hundred feet and more. The Simpson Desert, looked upon by the aboriginals as a place of death and evil spirits. Even the cattle were smart enough not to venture into the wilderness, grazing on the purple-flowering succulent, the parakeelya peculiar to the desert fringe.

'That's Paradise Pool over there,' Liza pointed, 'it's the most beautiful place!'

'It looks it.'

Blaise must have heard them, because he turned the jeep off the track and made down across the expanse of spiky grasses to the line of permanent deep water.

The heat had been heavy on the rolling savannahs, but under the dense green foliage, heavy in blossom and scent, the air was sparklingly cool and Laura would have given anything to dive into the beautiful emerald green pool.

'Watch it, it's a bit boggy,' said Blaise, lifting Liza in a short cut to the ground.

'I think I'll stay here, if you don't mind,' Claudia called to him with a little shudder, suggesting she had no intention of messing up her gleaming riding boots.

'What's that delicious scent?' Laura asked, her thick, silky hair freed from the hat, tumbling around her face.

'This here with the red berries,' Liza paused to show her. 'It's lovely, isn't it, like orange blossom or something, or even frangipanni.'

Until they descended to the shining sand no one spoke, so the extraordinary peace and quiet of the place produced its own magic. It was an extraordinarily soothing sight—the green trees, the sun-dappled shade and the unruffled sheet of water.

'I only wish I could go for a swim,' Laura found herself saying.

'Yes, wouldn't it be great!' Liza flung off her sandals and raced in to paddle, her sturdy little legs very brown beneath the short line of her red shorts. 'If Blaise wasn't here we could go in in the altogether.'

'Well, Miss Mallory?' he asked.

'I'm too flabbergasted to answer.'

A family coo-ee was wafting down the bank, an unmistakable call from Claudia for them all to return.

'May I bring Liza here?' Laura asked.

'Would you know how to find it?' He glanced at her, low-voiced and mocking.

'I think so.' She had never seen those dancing lights in his eyes before. Her flawless, creamy skin was warm with colour and her right hand was twirling a pink, fallen blossom. She looked very beautiful and rather tremulous, as though she found it a safeguard to have Liza around.

'Come in and paddle!' Liza called.

'Another time, little one,' Blaise said emphatically. 'Laura has quite a bit to see yet.'

The use of her name shook her and he narrowed his eyes a little as though he had guessed it. 'Do you think you could handle the jeep?' he asked.

'I'm sure of it.' She had to accept his outstretched hand to be pulled up the slope.

'I'll see first,' he said.

'Listen here, I'm not a baby!' Her eyes were enormous. 'I've had my licence for years.'

'I *am* sorry,' he gave her a sharp glance edged with amusement. 'When will you be twenty-one?'

'Next year,' she said shortly.

Claudia was quietly smouldering, though Laura recalled the significant information that she and Blaise had cooled off in the pool 'many a time'.

In the altogether? Laura found herself wondering with a humiliating vestige of jealousy. It surprised her and kept her quiet.

By the end of the tour she had seen a great deal and met a good many of the staff, including wives and the two sandy-haired children who had waved at the plane. Their names were Peter and Louise Noonan and their father was the head stockman.

'Cute little kids, aren't they?' Liza said to Laura, like another woman. 'When is Laura going to meet Sean?'

'He's working today,' said Blaise.

'Sean's nice,' Liza filled her in efficiently. 'He's our overseer. He's not married either.'

'I'm certain Miss Mallory will find him attractive,' said Blaise dryly.

He dropped them back at the house where Mrs Madden was waiting for them with chilled lime juice and old Mrs Hunter's request that Laura come to her sitting room after lunch.

'Me too?' Liza asked.

'Not you, young lady,' Mrs Madden gave Laura a wink. 'You can help me with the baking. A good little cook you'll make too.'

When Laura entered Mrs Hunter's memento-filled sitting room, the old lady looked up with a welcoming smile.

'Come in and sit down, my dear.' She moved rather slowly in her chair, obviously trying to set her book down.

'Here, let me take it.' Laura moved quickly, taking the thick leather-bound book out of the old lady's hand and placing it on a table that gleamed with silver-framed family photographs. Blaise was in the front line, man and boy, the expressions vastly separated.

'Thank, you, my dear. I suffer from arthritis, and some days are more difficult than others.'

'I'm sorry,' soothed Laura.

'I can see that—I knew you were a good girl at first sight. Still, I had the impression you were an unhappy one. Is there any way I can help you? Sometimes it helps to talk about our problems, examine them with a sympathetic friend.'

'Did your grandson not explain anything at all about me?' Laura asked.

'He merely said he'd found a suitable girl who came highly recommended. Howard Mitchell, I believe.'

'Our family solicitor,' Laura said in too calm a voice.

'Don't tell me, my dear, if you don't want to.'

'No, really, I'd like to.' Laura rested her hands together and looked down at them. 'It's this way, Mrs Hunter—my father died recently, very unexpectedly, and his will left everything to my stepmother and my four-year-old stepbrother. It rather changed my life. I'd been going along complacently, going to university, then the security fell out of my life. It was necessary for me to find a job.'

'Forgive me, my dear,' Mrs Hunter said gently, 'but was there some ill-feeling between you and your father? Something to explain his . . . unusual actions?'

'I loved my father dearly,' Laura said, 'and I thought he loved me. Of course I knew he loved Jamie more, but then he's my great favourite too. I miss him dreadfully.'

'Why, of course you do!' Wise old eyes were studying the girl attentively. 'I take it you and your stepmother are not compatible?'

'I suppose you could say she hates the sight of me, and I don't know why. I used to worry about it once. It made me miserable, but I never thought it was so serious that Paula would turn me out of the house.'

'Do you actually mean she *did*?' Mrs Hunter exclaimed, her fragile body in its lilac dress leaning forward.

'It was Mr Hunter who rescued me. He managed to be at the door the very morning Paula told me to leave. I don't think he really wanted me as governess to his daughter, but Uncle Howard rather persuaded him and my stepmother's ultimatum did the rest.'

'And your stepbrother, the little boy?'

'He must stay with his mother, of course. I must say she idolises him in her own way. She probably did it for him.'

'Did *what*?' The great diamond on the old lady's hand flashed.

'I don't really know,' Laura explained awkwardly. 'She admitted she complained of me to my father— deliberate mischief. It doesn't matter now.'

'And was there much money?' Mrs Hunter asked kindly.

'Certainly enough for all of us. Uncle Howard called my father a rich man.'

'I see.' The old lady leaned back in her chair. 'Your stepmother made no offer?'

'Oh, *no*!'

'How inhuman!'

'It doesn't matter,' Laura met that rather severe expression. 'It will all go to Jamie eventually.'

'It's you I'm thinking about,' Mrs Hunter said. 'I'm surprised at what you tell me, my dear, and pained. So you took this job?'

'I had to get away,' Laura explained.

'I can see that. And it hurts?'

Laura made an involuntary little motion of distress. 'I suppose we all have to lose someone we love. But Jamie is only four!'

'There, there!' the old lady spoke bracingly, but she too was moved. 'I've lived a long time and I've seen many things—things I've wished to change but couldn't, so I had to force myself to accept them. One day your stepbrother will want to see you and his mother won't be able to prevent him.'

'All those years,' Laura sighed. 'It's going to be hard.'

The old lady extended her hand. 'It will work out, you'll see. Now we won't discuss these painful things any longer. Tell me about yourself, your interests. Blaise tells me you're an art lover. . . .'

It wasn't until late that night, when she was preparing for bed, that Laura stopped to think that nobody in the household had ever mentioned Liza's mother. The tragedy was too near, she supposed, the strong emotions. Old Mrs Hunter, when Laura had remarked on the collection of family photographs in their beautiful antique sterling silver frames, had allowed her to look at many, but there was no remembrance of Virginia. Virginia, who had flown out of Hunter's Moon and never returned. It must have been hell—the crash, the notoriety and the speculation.

Tonight the moon was exquisite and Laura opened out her windows to their fullest extent. The full moon was enormous, golden, and she shook her hair back and tilted her head, half uttering an exclamation of pleasure.

When she looked down into the garden again, a man's tall figure was looking up at her and before she had a chance to move he made a faint bow in her direction. Back once more in the shadowed privacy of the room she stood flushed and trembling as though he had suddenly caught her naked instead of discreetly veiled by her nightdress. It wasn't pleasant to remind herself, but she had to. Blaise Hunter was the bitter survivor of one unhappy marriage, he was sheltering a handsome young woman called Claudia who would obviously give everything to have him as her private possession; two of Liza's governesses had made fools of themselves over him, crushes no doubt but still painful. Laura didn't intend to be another.

CHAPTER FIVE

By the end of the week they had settled into a routine with Liza's school work, working for three hours in the morning and two in the afternoon. A 'canny little soul', as Mrs Madden called her, Liza, in Laura's opinion, was considerably below standard with her work.

'Miss Grierson didn't explain it to me *that* way,' Liza said gratefully as she finally conquered a simple sum. 'I really hate school work, Laura. Don't you?' Liza was now puzzling over the next one.

'It will get easier, dear, don't worry. Well, no—that's not the way!' Patiently Laura explained the technique of division again.

'Why can't we go for a swim?' sighed Liza. 'It's so flaming hot! Shall I tell you a funny thing?'

'After you've written down the right answer.'

'Miss Grierson used to wear these teeny bikinis,' prevaricated Liza.

'Did she have a good figure?' Laura asked.

'Unfortunately, Blaise used to say, no. But it was really comic the way she used to get up early and go for a swim when Blaise was around. She must have had a dozen costumes. Annie and I used to go into fits of giggles!'

'Poor Miss Grierson. Evidently she didn't teach you how to do these sums.'

'She was always keeping an eye out for Blaise.'

'And who was your governess before that?' Somebody had to account for Liza's slow progress.

'Miss Knowles. She had red-gold curls.'

'And did she get up early in the morning?'

'No, she was very quiet, but Annie said still waters run deep.'

'Sometimes,' said Laura. 'Listen, pet, before we make much progress you really will have to know your tables.'

'Oh, goodness!' Liza was very despondent on hearing this. 'Couldn't we finish these off later, Laura? As Blaise would say, at a more favourable time.'

'It won't be any different then. Buck up, we'll have a swim later. This afternoon.'

Mid-afternoon Liza took off like a migrating bird. 'You really are a serious teacher,' she told Laura as they took a run out to Paradise Pool.

'That's what I'm here for.'

'Claudia keeps wanting to know what we're doing.'

'Then we'll write her an essay,' said Laura.

'She's really strange, don't you think?' Liza's blue

eyes were very bright under the shade of her hat. 'Of course, she's in love with Blaise.'

Who isn't? Laura thought sardonically.

'Anyway,' Liza confided, 'there's no use her looking in that direction. Blaise will never get married again.'

'Why not, dear?' Laura felt a flash of sadness.

'We think it's a terrible idea and I detest Claudia. Even Aunty Judith is much nicer to me than that.'

It didn't make sense. Claudia wanted to marry Blaise, yet she made no effort to befriend his young daughter. Even Paula had tried to do that in the early days, bringing Laura little presents and planning outings that never quite came off. Claudia, inexplicably, was making no such effort, though she was as sweet as bush honey with Blaise.

'Oh, this is magic!' Laura exclaimed as they came down on the jewelled pool. The sun fell in broad chinks through the lacy canopy of acacias and the air was fresh and green like the earth after a shower.

'Beat you in!' Liza cried.

'Perhaps.' Laura was pleased now she hadn't brought a bikini. A serious swimmer, she preferred a one-piece, but it was the very latest one-piece, beautifully cut and infinitely flattering.

They had a glorious time—Liza swam well enough, but not strongly, and after a little while Laura began to correct the child's action, and here, at least, she had an apt pupil. Even in one lesson Liza showed a marked improvement.

They were lazing on the sand when an attractive male voice called out to them. Liza whirled up, but Laura, caught with the straps of her swimsuit untied, had to take her time.

'I suppose this is Miss Mallory, the new governess?' The young man looking down at her wasn't bothering to hide his interest in her or her body. He was studying her with amazing openness and a decided hint of astonishment.

'Come on, Liza, introduce me to your friend.'

Liza liked the role. 'This is Sean, Laura. We were wondering when you were going to get back.'

Sean, a man of action, seized Laura's hand. 'Are you as clever as you're beautiful?' he grinned.

'Oh, yes.' Liza began to preen on Laura's behalf. 'She's taught me more in a week than I've learned in years!'

'And that's *something*!' Sean gave Liza's head a shake. 'I haven't got used to Miss Mallory yet.'

But Laura had had enough attention. She bent down and retrieved her brilliantly patterned beach sarong, tying it around her in a long skirt. 'The pool is quite wonderful here, isn't it?' she said conversationally.

'Remind me to join you for a swim.' He was a very attractive young man, light brown hair bleached to blond, above average height, whipcord-thin, with sherry-coloured eyes. They were very aware of women, but he seemed so good-natured it was difficult to take offence.

'Hear about the tragedy?' he suddenly asked Liza, realising that Laura was far more reserved than Miss Grierson, for instance.

'What tragedy?' Liza was all ears.

'Picked up a couple of tourists in a creek bend, just over the border. They took the wrong turning and left their car.'

'Dead?' Laura asked soberly.

'Yes,' Sean answered in a voice that said, what else? 'A trip that started out as an adventure. When will people learn? They were totally dehydrated.'

'How terrible!' the two girls exclaimed together.

'Terrible, yes, and unnecessary. The desert isn't a playground. It must be treated with the utmost respect.'

'I suppose people just don't realise,' Laura said sadly. She made a movement and the full sun fell on her thick mane of hair. 'I suppose we'd better get going, Liza.'

'Don't rush off because of me,' said Sean, with a faintly wry smile on his face. 'You'll have to forgive me for staring, ma'am. We have a problem with a shortage of women out here and you'd be remarkable anywhere.'

'I think he likes you, Laura,' Liza beamed.

'When you're not encouraging young Liza here with her lessons, I'd like to take you riding,' Sean told Laura. 'There are heaps of fascinating things to see.'

'Laura doesn't ride very well.' Liza gave a little cough.

'I'll soon teach her.'

'You couldn't teach *me*!'

'That's different.'

'I *am* surprised at you, Sean,' Liza said.

She sounded so droll both adults burst out laughing, and that was the way Blaise Hunter found them as he rode down the bank.

'So here you are, Sean,' he called out rather testily.

Sean looked curiously mortified. 'Just came down to say hello to the girls.'

'I hope they're appreciative.' Sitting his gleaming jet-black horse, Blaise looked as if he wasn't going to suffer any more delay. A vertical line was between his winged black brows and he looked impatient, intolerant and as arrogant as the devil. 'I want you to lay that new man off. Do it right away. I won't have anyone on the station who illtreats stock.'

'What, Benson?' Sean stifled an inappropriate exclamation.

'Benson.' The black eyes under the silver-grey Stetson looked little short of furious. 'I told you when you hired him to watch him.'

'Right, Boss, I'll get on it. Some of them are like that.'

'Not here, they're not!'

'No.' Sean turned back to Laura with a faint effort. 'See you later, Miss Mallory.'

'Sean.' She felt sorry for him and she didn't know his other name. She spoke as she always did, gently, but her voice seemed to have a thrill in it; a feeling of helplessness really, but Blaise Hunter obviously interpreted it differently, for his black eyes narrowed in enigmatic appraisal. Her swimsuit was black, halter-necked with a deep V, and it contrasted beautifully with her hair and her skin and the brilliant jersey skirt that clung to her like a skin.

'Are you angry, Blaise?' Liza was asking.

At once the current of hostility left his face. 'Not with you, Betsy. Enjoy your swim?'

'Oh, it was great!' Smiling radiantly, Liza climbed the bank. 'Laura is such a terrific swimmer. She seems to do *everything* well.'

'Undoubtedly.' Blaise Hunter flashed Laura a glance that was more critical than praising. 'I'm very broad-minded, Miss Mallory, but I should warn you I don't approve of staff liaisons. A man can get too distracted to do his job. Or he can get careless and ignore trouble.'

'Who are you referring to, Mr Hunter?' Colour spread over the cream of her skin.

'I don't have to spell it out.'

'I think you do!' She had reached him now, trembling with humiliation and the unfairness of it all.

Incredibly he swooped, and with steel arms and steel wrists lifted her into the saddle and held her in front of him with one arm locked across her body.

'*Oh!*' Her heart fluttered madly in fright.

'Heck, Blaise!' Liza looked up at them both incredulously.

'I'm joking, of course.'

'You frightened the life out of Laura,' Liza pointed out briskly, then suddenly gave way to a gale of hilarity. 'That was the funniest thing I ever saw!'

Laura, however, sat transfixed. His arm was beneath her breasts, his warm breath on her cheek and the shock of it was unbearable. She knew she was shaking. She knew, holding her so closely, he was aware of it, and she had to muffle the moan that rose to her throat. If he had meant to unsettle her it had been a great victory. If she only moved her head, twisted it back a little . . . it was the same dark rush of desire that had seized her that other time, the trembling, fearful excitement that was driving her half crazy.

'Take her for a ride,' Liza called. 'Gosh, Laura, you look like a captive princess!'

'I feel more like a slave!' She had to find her voice, make light of the matter, with Liza staring up at them, her head full of Gothic tales.

'And not particularly aching to get away.'

She had absolutely nothing to say to Blaise when her traitorous body left him in no doubt. While Liza clapped her hands in excitement, he wheeled the stallion around, sent it swiftly up the slope and as the little girl ran after them put the magnificent animal through a galloping semicircle.

'Marvellous!' Liza shouted delightedly. Laura wasn't in the least afraid, she thought. In fact she

looked every bit as much at home on a horse as Blaise
did. Perhaps it wasn't so frightening after all!

As for Laura, she felt dizzy with delight, longing to
fly off across the distant, rolling savannah, somewhere beyond the shimmering horizon while legions of
brilliantly coloured, flashing birds accompanied them
on their flight. At no other time of her life had she had
such moments of intense pleasure, such a gush of excitement it was like a raging in the blood. And there
was more to astonish her.

Instead of reining the horse in some little distance
from Liza, they cantered into the miraculous shade,
where he grasped the shining mass of her hair and
tilted her face back towards him.

'You *can* ride, can't you? I can feel it in the movement of your body.'

The tug on her hair, the slight pain of it, parted her
soft mouth. Their faces were only inches apart, their
bodies touching, so many sensations crowding in on
her and most of all the exquisite awareness. . . .

'No!' he said harshly, and the hand on her hair
tightened so the ready tears sprang into her eyes.

Some violence prowled in him and above all one
thing. He wanted to kiss her, but there was no joy in
the knowledge.

'You're hurting me,' she whispered, not frightened,
but shaking like a leaf.

'Oh, you mean you noticed?'

His eyes, so intently on her, were bewildering,
dazzling, and she, too, remarked every little thing
about him . . . the fine grain of his bronzed skin, the
emphatic black of his brows and lashes, the clean bone
structure of his face, the arrangement of muscle, the
way the outline of his mouth was so distinctly edged
. . . *everything* . . . it gave her the most violent pleasure,

yet her body seemed unable to withstand the pressure.

She reached back slowly and put her hand over his. 'Please?'

'After all, I didn't plan to do anything. I didn't even know you'd be down at the pool.' The brilliant glance was insolent and mocking at once. Blaise dropped his hand and she was free to turn away, but it was the most stupendous effort, and he laughed aloud, an unkind laugh that acknowledged her surrender. 'Let's go back to Liza, shall we?'

In that moment Laura knew she was in love with him. Only one thing saved her. It had never been intentional and she had plenty of pride, in her own manner.

She had somehow expected him to shelve the subject of her riding, but after dinner that night, before he retired to the privacy of his study, he told her to report to the stables complex at six o'clock in the morning. He told her this without a backward glance, but Claudia, coming in from the veranda, caught his words and visibly tautened.

'Oh, Miss Mallory, one moment.'

'Yes?' Turning slowly, Laura had plenty of time to absorb Claudia's hostility.

'Do come out and sit in the cool. The sky is glorious tonight.'

'Well, perhaps for a little while, but I have letters to write.'

'Really?' Claudia gave her a tight smile. 'Some boyfriend or other?'

'Letters home.'

'Secretive thing, aren't you?' Claudia, the taller by an inch or so, looked down at the pure profile. 'I can't remember your saying a single thing about your family.'

'I didn't think you were interested.'

'Oh, but I *am*. We all are.' Claudia sank into a comfortable chair and indicated another. The honoured guest to an employee and don't-jolly-well-forget-it.

Laura sat down and stared up at the night sky. It was blazing with stars ... Alpha, Centauri, Sirius, Orion, exceptionally bright and clear in the uniquely clean, unpolluted air. The Milky Way was densely strewn with jewels, the home of the Aboriginal ancients, and the Southern Cross hung over the house like an omen.

'Perfect!' she breathed. 'I don't think I've ever seen such a fabulous sky.'

'Oh, lord, our skies are like this all the time,' Claudia shrugged impatiently. 'I'm longing to see how much progress you've been making with Liza.'

'Quite a lot,' said Laura, and let it go at that.

'One of these mornings I'll join you in the classroom.'

'I'm afraid Liza might lose her concentration if you did that.'

'Are you telling me not to come?' Claudia drew in a rasping breath.

'What I meant was,' Laura returned firmly, 'Liza would become nervous and we would lose valuable time.'

'How silly! You've all the time in the world.'

'Not if I'm going to bring Liza up to the required standard, and I'm determined to do that.'

'Really, Miss Mallory,' Claudia gave a forced laugh, 'you quite bowl me over! Do you mean to tell me Liza is as bad as all that?'

'It's more a case of she hadn't been particularly well taught,' Laura explained.

'I don't know what the devil you're talking about,' said Claudia, with the face of shock. 'My own sister interviewed the last two girls and their qualifications were excellent.'

Laura gave a little shrug. 'It's possible to be well qualified but without the capacity for teaching.'

'And you have it, I suppose?' Claudia made no attempt to soften the sarcasm.

'I like it, you see. Now, if you'll excuse me, I really must write those letters.'

'I wouldn't dream of excusing you,' Claudia said sharply. 'I insist you tell me. Did you suggest these riding lessons?' Her imperious, rather long-boned face took on an expression of extreme hauteur.

'Not a bit,' Laura told her, and stood up. 'It was entirely Mr Hunter's idea.'

'Now that I can't imagine,' Claudia said. 'The sensible plan would have been to leave the whole thing to me. I'm well able to show you the rudiments of riding if you're after a little diversion. You've left it far too late to even begin to ride well. You could even find it difficult.'

'I'm determined to bear with it.'

'Then I'll join you at the stables,' Claudia told her shortly.

There was a dry cough behind them and Steven Hunter sauntered out on to the verandah, glass in hand. 'Don't tell me you two are squabbling?'

Claudia looked back at him in feigned astonishment. 'My dear Steven, one doesn't squabble with a governess!'

'Quarrel, then.' Steven stood his ground. 'You're not going, are you, Miss Mallory? I haven't had one significant conversation with you since you arrived.'

'She has letters to write,' Claudia told him darkly.

'Frankly, I feel like a turn around the garden.' He tossed the contents of his glass off and looked around for somewhere to put it down. 'Do join me, Miss Mallory. You seem to have made a thoroughly good impression on the whole household, except Claudia here.' The malice was quite forthright.

'It's not my nature to be easily impressed,' Claudia retorted ironically. 'To tell you the truth, I think Miss Mallory is beginning to give herself a few airs.'

'I think you're wrong, but since she's not the only one. . . .'

'You certainly have it in for me lately, haven't you, Steven?' Claudia lunged to her feet, her tall, athletic body coiled like a tigress about to spring.

'I expect you know the reasons for that,' Steven Hunter retorted almost peacefully, and put out his hand. 'Please join me, Miss Mallory. I'd like to know a little more about the girl who's become Liza's immediate favourite.'

It was impossible to refuse and Laura walked down into the garden with him, feeling a sensuous pleasure in the beauty of the night and the boronia-scented breeze.

'How are you finding Liza as a pupil?' Steven asked her when they had walked a little way.

'Better every day. At the beginning it was a little hard to hold her attention.'

'Nice little kid!' Steven said with the strangest note of pity. 'If we were going to be the only human beings you saw I wouldn't tell you this, but there'll be plenty of outsiders flying in and out of the station within the next couple of months and they won't allow you to remain in ignorance for very long.'

'I beg your pardon?' Even before Laura heard it she flinched as though preparing for the blow.

'I'm surprised Claudia hasn't told you, in her callous way.'

Laura said nothing, but her fists closed tight, her nails biting into the skin.

'I expect you've heard how Liza's mother was killed?' he asked quietly, standing still and staring out over the tops of the trees.

'Actually I've heard very little,' Laura didn't glance at him. 'Neither did I consider it my business.'

'None of us can hide from it,' he answered rather bitterly. 'If you're to help Liza, there are some things you must know.'

'Mr Hunter didn't want me to know them,' Laura protested unhappily. Hear secrets about that proud man!

'I haven't heard Blaise mention Virginia since he found her out.'

'Oh, please, Mr Hunter,' she put her fingers on his arm, 'you must understand that my loyalty is to your brother. I can't stand here gossiping about him.'

'My dear young lady, I'm not asking you to. We're having a serious conversation.'

'Surely I can learn what I have to in good time. Mrs Hunter, your grandmother, sees me every day.'

'Yes, and she's carried the burden a long time. My grandmother is no meek little old lady. She's a woman of fierce family pride. But you can't stop people talking, and Liza bears so little resemblance to her mother there's no conceivable cover.'

'Of course you're telling me Liza is not your brother's child.' Laura could not bear to drag this on.

'Heaven knows, the whole countryside knows!' he groaned distractedly.

'And does Liza?'

'Who the hell is going to break it to her?' Steven

Hunter demanded. 'Poor little soul, as though it's *her* fault!'

Laura put her head down and closed her eyes.

'I've upset you, haven't I?' He peered at her in the velvet gloom.

'Look at the danger of the situation,' she said, almost sharply. 'If her family isn't going to tell Liza, somebody else will! After all, you were obviously worried about my hearing.'

'Liza is a child,' he reminded her. 'No one willingly hurts a child, no matter how much they like to talk.'

'But, good heavens, she could overhear!' Laura was vividly, painfully reminded of all the snippets of conversation Liza had recorded so smartly.

'No one will tell Liza for a while,' Steven Hunter maintained thinly.

'I can't think it's wise to let it go. For one thing, she adores her father.'

'Her father was a station hand,' Steven Hunter told her flatly. 'You don't believe me?'

'I. . . .' Laura held a hand to her rippling throat.

'So beautiful, Virginia, but she was really frightful. Of course they saw one another so briefly, so infrequently, it was really an arranged marriage. Blaise had the station to think of . . . yes, indeed, a great heritage. He thought Virginia was as beautiful as she looked and there didn't seem any good reason for him not to marry her and start a family. Heirs for Hunter's Moon. Her own family were pressing for it to happen. They had the money and we had the money and the grandeur. It was thought to be the most desirable match possible, and Virginia was so sweet to everyone.' A contemptuous smile came to his mouth. 'It's a terrible thing, I know, to speak ill of the dead, but Virginia managed to

alienate us all within a couple of months after they
returned from their honeymoon. I don't know that
Blaise ever *loved* her. He was certainly *in* love with
her, but that soon came to an end. Virginia was that
odd thing in a woman, promiscuous. She used to say it
was because Blaise was never there, and he *wasn't* after
he found out about the first, careless affair. My grandmother thought she couldn't help it. It was a sort of
illness. She couldn't stand the isolation of the station
and every trip she made, and they became increasingly
more frequent, she had to find blind adoration. Easy,
for a while, with her looks.'

From the bitterness of his voice, Laura suspected he
had his own painful memories. 'And Liza's father?'

'A nice, ordinary bloke. Virginia would have seduced
him in a minute.'

'But surely, when Mr Hunter found out . . .?'

'Virginia would dare anything, believe me,' Steven
assured her. 'She seemed to have no sense of honour,
no balance, but the bloke did. He got out just as quick
as he could—hitched a ride with the mail.'

'And you never heard from him afterwards?'

'Not in a way that made us happy. As a matter of
fact, he met a violent death. He was taken by a croco-
dile right off the bank where he was camping in the
Gulf country. It was all so horrible it made the papers.
Virginia, six months pregnant, just made a sick joke.'

'She *must* have been ill,' Laura murmured.

'Yes. I didn't want to have to tell you this story,
Miss Mallory, but you seem like a girl who can be
trusted. My brother is a sort of hero figure to most
people, which is just fine when there's nothing to hide
but my family hate Virginia for what she did to us.'

'No one can destroy your own good name,' Laura
told him.

'Some sure try to—the ones who are jealous of what we've got.'

'All the more reason to prepare Liza now.' Laura lifted her head to look at him.

'I expect you're right,' he said in a controlled voice, 'but who wants to torture the poor little devil? No one willingly. Not a soul. She's the innocent victim and she hasn't got a lot of things going for her. I mean, she's such a plain little kid, isn't she? A little stranger. In the beginning I didn't know how Blaise could bear to look at her, but I guess he's not the man to take his anger out on a defenceless child. Besides, Virginia rejected her from the beginning, untouched by any kind of pity or maternal feeling. There would have been no child at all, only she was too late discovering it.'

Laura took a few steps away from him and sat down on a stone garden seat.

'Most people have secrets, Miss Mallory,' Steven Hunter told her in a hollow voice. 'Don't take it as a personal blow.'

'Only I care for Liza,' Laura sighed.

'Why not?' He sat down beside her. 'You're a compassionate girl. I even feel comfortable with you, and I'm not exactly happy myself. My own marriage isn't working out the way I wanted, and I can see a procession of empty years ahead. You see, I haven't got Blaise's positive quality, the strength and the power. He spares himself nothing and everyone respects him. I became what I am because my name is Hunter and my life is here.'

'You don't love it?' Laura asked in amazement.

'I do and I don't. Certainly it's not the centre of my life as it always has been with Blaise and my father. The truth is, I'm not cut out to be a cattle baron. I just agree with everything Blaise says.'

'So what would you do if you had the chance?' she asked him.

'Oh, damn well anything.' Steven twined his long fingers together, then placed his arms behind his head. 'I think I'd like to write a book. Good adventure stuff.'

'Well, why not do it?'

He sighed deeply, 'I work the whole day and I'm too damned tired at night. Writing a best-seller, or even a clever book takes time and concentration. I've got plenty to say, plenty of background material, but I haven't got the guts to meet what I really want to do head-on.'

'And have you spoken to your brother?'

'About writing? What a silly question! Blaise would think I was crazy.'

'Surely it's crazier to live unfulfilled?'

'Don't worry about it, Miss Mallory. It's not important. I'll go on being Blaise's younger brother— good bloke, but not a bloke to take seriously. I know how everyone feels ... the men. Even if Blaise had been the second son he would still have been the Boss. You know, made in the feudal mould. Everyone looks up to him, the regal air. I could hate him but I don't. I love and admire him—I admit it openly.' Steven sighed. 'Blaise should get married again, but I doubt if he'll ever soften. Virginia didn't break his heart, but she almost killed his respect for women.'

'But surely, so highly intelligent, he realises one bad experience. . . .'

'Couldn't happen again?' He couldn't control himself not to interrupt her. 'You've been in the house long enough to see Claudia is very interested in him, and Claudia is such a bitch!' His voice, softer and lighter than his brother's, grew angry. 'Claudia wants this house to be hers. And lord knows she's always wanted Blaise. He's that rare man, so many women work so hard to get him to notice them, it's small wonder he gets bored. What's he got anyway?' he gave Laura a lopsided smile. 'All the girls used to think *I* was so handsome until Blaise finished that at a stroke. Anyway, all the gods weren't present at his birth. His marriage was a total disaster in a man who had always achieved perfection.'

'We're all human, that's the point,' Laura told him.

'Yes.' He gave her a glance of liking and respect. 'I only wish my brother had met a girl like you, but these days he doesn't think a girl like you exists.'

It was a statement Laura couldn't answer, so she remained silent.

'You're a good listener, aren't you, Miss Laura Mallory? You don't press anything. I was dreading the chance that you might learn the whole story from Claudia. I knew Judy wouldn't tell you. She feels exactly as I do, but Claudia would make it out all uglier than it was. You see, she hated Virginia. No one was more pleased than Claudia when it all happened. When we learned, beyond doubt, that it was Virginia's plane that had crashed, Claudia saw her great chance. But nothing's happened. Blaise doesn't want her at all and to my mind she's worn out her welcome. She only arrives and my wife turns into somebody else. Say no more.'

All he had told her kept Laura headachey and uneasily awake for many long hours. What an atrocious story, and an added danger to come. How could little Liza accept the shattering news that the man she adored wasn't her father? Where were the grandparents, the *real* grandparents, Virginia's family—didn't they want her?

Somehow she knew the answer. They didn't. Had Liza possessed her mother's physical beauty it might have been supposed she *was* Blaise Hunter's child. It would have gained her importance in the Moorhouses' eyes. But Liza had turned out to be that impossible thing, the image of somebody else; a nobody no one wanted to talk about.

When she arrived in the quadrangle of the stables complex only two young Aboriginal boys were about.

''Mornin', miss.' Both of them seemed slightly taken aback, the older lad scratching his curly head in confusion, though he was determined to do the best he could. 'Can I help you, miss?'

'Is Mr Hunter here?' she asked.

'Well . . . well . . . the *Boss* was.'

'And when was that?' Laura was miserably aware that she was over twenty minutes late.

'Seems like a long time ago, was it?' the older boy asked his friend, who failed to reply.

'Was Miss Stewart here?' Laura persisted, with a certain firmness.

'Yes, miss, but she spoke to the Boss an' went back to da house.'

'Thank you.' Laura shrugged and smiled. 'Would there be a horse I could take out? I'm dressed for riding, so I think I'll do so.'

'There's Rebel.'

'Rebel?' the other suddenly crowed scornfully. 'She can't ride that!'

'Maybe I could have a look at her,' Laura was now curious.

'She temperamental, you know,' the first boy drawled laconically.

'That's good,' Laura said briskly. 'Think you can

saddle her up for me?'

'Oh, my goodness!'

It took a few more minutes of persuasion before a high-class-looking chestnut was led out, looking decidedly sulky.

'Good rider, miss?' the first boy asked with a certain amount of consternation.

'I'll manage,' Laura smiled at him. 'What's your name?'

'Albert, miss.'

'Well, Albert,' Laura ordered pleasantly, 'why don't you just find me a saddle? Rebel looks wound up and a good gallop will straighten her out.'

It was obvious from the expression on the boy's glossy black face that he disagreed, but he wasn't going to argue. 'Where are you goin', miss?' he asked.

'Not far,' she replied honestly. 'Just enough to give Rebel a little exercise.'

As soon as she mounted the graceful mare, Rebel gave a good, hefty buck, but as Laura had been expecting it, it was not the disaster it might have been. In fact Laura was feeling a little lift of elation after the depression and the sleeplessness of the night before. Nothing could be plainer that Rebel wasn't sweet-natured, but Laura felt certain the mare would be a wonderful, impetuous ride.

And that was how it turned out. Rebel, a moody, feminine creature, loved to gallop, so Laura, once they were out on the grasslands, gave the hot-tempered mare her head.

It might have been a cross-country, so madly did they charge at it. 'Oh, *beautiful*!' Laura cried, and her delight was for the mare. Rebel wasn't only wonderful to look at, she was a beautiful mover. In fact, Laura had never ridden a faster horse in her life. They went fearlessly, Laura talking to the horse all the way. She had always felt at home high up on a horse's back, and horses, of course, even temperamental beauties like Rebel, were smart enough to know it and act accordingly.

The birds and a bunch of far-off grazing cattle weren't the only ones to remark their effortless flight.

'Who the hell is that?' Blaise Hunter demanded shortly of his foreman, his black eyes glinting oddly.

Ginger-haired Ted Dunn's humorous mouth fell open. 'Sure, it's the girl, the new governess.'

No one else said a word, sitting their good steady work horses while a slip of a horse-handling girl rode that gleaming chestnut rogue, Rebel.

'She's managing her beautifully,' Ted commented with a grin. 'They're as good a sight as any to watch. Hi there, Miss Mallory!'

Of course when she saw them, she had to rein in, the long minutes of uncomplicated pleasure beginning to dim. The small group of men were looking frankly admiring, but Blaise Hunter's autocratic dark face wore another expression altogether.

'So I've found you!' she addressed him a little shyly. 'I'm sorry I missed you this morning, but I slept in.'

Blaise Hunter didn't answer but turned to nod to his foreman. 'Thanks, Ted. You might comb the lignum for some of those strays.'

'See you.' Ted tipped his hat and grinned at Laura rather sheepishly. 'You're a mighty fine rider, Miss Mallory. You should be proud.'

From the flash in Blaise Hunter's black eyes she knew he was just itching to make a sharp remark, but he waited until the men had moved away. 'Why didn't you tell me you were an experienced rider?' he asked, and his face was stern.

'I told you I could ride.'

'Your *exact* words were that you could only just stay on.'

'Behave yourself, Rebel!' The mare was moving restlessly.

'What else do you lie about?' Blaise demanded.

'I didn't lie at all. I just gave you a silly answer.'

'Why?'

'Because you always act so damned superior!' There, it was out, her tongue loosened in upset and outrage.

'While you, Miss Mallory,' he returned curtly, 'are playing a decidedly odd role. Are you now my brother's confidante?'

The cynicism in his eyes dismayed her. 'I beg your pardon?'

'Get the mare in hand,' he snapped back at her, ignoring her incensed tone.

'Yes, my lord.' Not surprisingly Rebel was reacting to the human tension, backing, head tossing, and Laura bent to calming her immediately. 'That's my girl! *Good* girl,' she murmured encouragingly, fighting the fractious animal with her hands and knees.

Incredibly Rebel stopped and Laura lifted her head, took a deep breath and met Blaise Hunter's cynical gaze, a little frightened by the expressions that played across his handsome face.

'You're a clever girl,' he drawled.

It sounded more like an insult than a compliment. 'Only about horses,' she said quietly. 'I've been awfully wrong about people.'

'What people?' he challenged her, his eyes coldly brilliant. 'Tell me, I want to know.'

'You *do* know,' she told him wearily. 'Would you excuse me, Mr Hunter? I have a terrible headache.'

And now she had, elation replaced by reaction from the night before.

'I'd be glad to.' He looked straight into her shadowed eyes.

'How cruel, the way you put it.' Her voice sounded muffled with a kind of pain.

'But then I'm a difficult, cruel man.'

'In some things,' she agreed shakily, and sank her small white teeth in her bottom lip.

This, apparently, pushed him over the edge. His face tautened and the lines from nostril to mouth became more deeply pronounced. 'If you're going,' he said stingingly, 'go now.'

Colour rushed up under her skin and her silvery-grey eyes dilated. How she hated his look of glittery arrogance! She wheeled the mare's head around, touched her with her heels and Rebel obliged, settling in quickly to her long, springy stride.

A man like Blaise Hunter made ordinary communications impossible. Laura didn't think she would want to speak to him again.

CHAPTER SIX

AT the end of the week Clive Stewart flew in to collect his elder daughter.

'Not before time!' Mrs Madden clucked in Laura's ear. It had been a week of many disruptions, much rudeness and a fairly serious argument between the two sisters, during which Judith had broken out of her habitual ennui to champion Laura against her sister's caustic attack. Now, with Claudia gone, Judith had become much less her sister's look-alike and even obeyed the sudden impulse to establish a rapport with the new governess.

'You really are a beautiful rider,' she told Laura warmly as they spelled their horses at a waterhole. 'I always thought Claudia was the best woman rider I've ever seen, but you give me more pleasure to watch. I suppose it's because you seem to actually enjoy it more than Claudia. She has a rather different approach.'

Laura murmured, in actual fact more engrossed in watching a great, floating eagle. With its seven-foot wing span and three-inch talons she knew it was quite capable of killing and carrying off a medium-sized kangaroo, and there were quite a few in the vicinity.

'As to what you've done for Liza,' Judith continued, 'please don't take my sister's comments to heart. I have to apologise for Claudia. In some of her moods she's barely civil, and in your case downright unfair. For myself and Steven, I want to say an extravagant thank-you. Liza is much, much happier since you've arrived, and she's shown me all those filled-up exercise books!'

'She's coming on nicely,' Laura flashed the other girl a quick smile.

'Steven mentioned something to you about Liza, didn't he?' Judith asked, with a serious look in her dark eyes.

'We did discuss Liza, yes,' Laura said cautiously.

'I suppose he was absolutely right to tell you,' Judith said. 'He must be right and it must be for the best. Lord knows you'll find out from some unscrupulous person.' There was a kind of pain in Judith's well-bred voice and a great embarrassment. 'Poor little soul, I feel for her when I'm not actually so . . . angry. It was Virginia's way of trying to bring Blaise down. I'm telling you this, too, Laura, because like Steven, I feel we can trust you, and quite simply you're a person who really cares about children. It's difficult to talk about what Virginia was,' she went on. 'She was fabulous to look at, but she had no self-respect at all. She hurt this family dreadfully, and her own. Her parents are such stern, cold people and their life style is absolutely beyond reproach.' Judith released a jerky breath, her expression that of a woman under pressure. 'In the beginning she went all out for Blaise and her family wanted the marriage as much as she did. Everyone believed it would work. The only thing was, Virginia couldn't take sharing Blaise with the station. She wanted him with her every minute of the day and night. She wanted him like a starving person, but of course, it was impossible. You know how Blaise works, his commitments, his business trips, the work he does for the industry, his total dedication to Hunter's Moon. He was bred to it, and besides, it's *in* him. I'm not suggesting he didn't try very hard to make his marriage work, he did, but the station had to be first on his list of priorities. Any grazier's wife can tell you that, but usually they're dedicated to the common interest. My own mother is one and Claudia, for all her high-handedness, would accept what Blaise has to do. Virginia didn't, wouldn't, couldn't. When she lost Blaise's love and respect she went all out to destroy him. It was a terrible love-hate where no side could win and Virginia could only dash herself to pieces. *I* don't think she had as many affairs as she claimed. Really if you knew her you couldn't conceive of her wanting anyone else but Blaise. I'm convinced she wasn't wanton, but she had to have a man's admiration, that's to say every man that came into sight, like you and I need the air we're breathing. It must be terrible to feel like that, something you have no control over.'

'You pitied her, didn't you?' Laura asked quietly.

'Pitied her. Despised her. She would never listen to one word of advice. I really don't like to talk about it, but I *have* to. What it did to all of us.'

'To Liza.'

'Yes.' Judith raised her head and looked sightlessly at the quivering blue line of mirage; phantom lakes. 'We've all spent sleepless nights thinking about Liza. It would have been so much easier if she'd looked like Virginia. Virginia's people might have accepted her for one thing, but seeing she looks like her . . . her father, they've closed their doors on her. To the Moorhouses, Liza simply doesn't exist.'

'How dreadful!' said Laura, appalled.

'They might have loved her had she looked like Virginia,' Judith added.

'A selfish kind of loving, surely? I can only love you if you're pretty and clever and recognisably one of our own.'

'A lot of people are like that,' Judith answered. 'Physical beauty is important, and it's such an anguish that Liza is so plain.'

'Yet you're telling me a story where great physical beauty didn't count.'

'Don't get angry at me,' Judith pleaded. 'I try very hard to be nice to Liza, but one can't see anything of anybody's family in her. She must be totally her father's people.'

'Just ordinary country folk.'

'She adores Blaise,' Judith said simply.

'Yes, she does.'

'She could never want to hear he's not her father. That would be like destroying her world.'

There was one thing Laura could do for her, that old

Mrs Hunter had come to love. Always a great reader, her failing eyesight had brought about a change in her reading habits, but once she mentioned it in the course of conversation Laura immediately offered to read to her.

It started casually one evening with Shirley Hazzard's *The Transit of Venus* and went on easily from there. Laura had the ideal voice for reading, low and melodious and naturally full of expression, and both of them had come to enjoy these companionable evening sessions.

'You don't mind?' Mrs Hunter asked her, when Laura offered to read on to Chapter Ten. 'It's a very engrossing book altogether and you're bringing it alive.'

'She has another book out, I believe—*The Bay of Noon*. I must get it for you. Now, where was I?' Laura traced her forefinger under the printed line. . . . 'In these warm days, Tertia came and went. . . .'

Twenty minutes later, coming in the open doorway of his grandmother's spacious sitting room, Blaise Hunter looked beyond Laura's, shining downbent head to his grandmother. She was leaning back in her chair, eyes closed, her expression blissfully transported. Neither woman had noticed him and Laura's limpid voice was conjuring up considerable atmosphere . . . 'and Ted Tice saw that these two had, perhaps that very day, been lovers.'

'I scarcely like to interrupt.' He walked across to his grandmother, bent his tall frame over her and kissed her on the temple. 'Hi!'

'Oh, darling, how are you?' the old lady caught at his hand. 'What did Viv Langston want?'

'To buy a parcel of our land.'

'And what did you tell him?'

'No.'

'Precisely.' The old lady chuckled. 'I hear he's picked up some around Baskin Downs?'

'His partner is behind it.'

'George made the wrong decision,' she pronounced.

'He needed the money urgently.' Blaise Hunter turned his head and his brilliant gaze swept Laura's face and her gracefully curled up body. 'You two are making yourselves very comfortable here,' he observed smoothly.

His grandmother laughed peacefully. 'I'm sure I wouldn't know what to do without Laura now. She's opened a whole new world to me, or rather the old world that was closed.'

'What do you mean?' The winged brows came together.

'I mean, dear boy, Laura reads to me, and so beautifully. My old eyes weren't taking the strain.'

'I didn't realise,' he said, looking very much as though he blamed himself for missing anything connected with the well-being of his grandmother.

'It was nothing, darling,' the old lady sat, composed and smiling, 'you know you think of everything for my comfort, only Laura was smart enough to think of reading to me, and believe me, she has me hanging on every word!'

'Didn't I tell you you were a clever girl?' he drawled.

'You did,' Laura said uncertainly, then blinked to break his disturbing gaze.

'Did you want anything, darling?' Mrs Hunter asked.

'A few words with Miss Mallory here.' The black eyes brushed Laura's startled face.

'Then take her off.' Mrs Hunter turned the kindest
face on Laura. 'Thank you so much, my dear. I'm very
grateful to you.'

'But I enjoy it as much as you do.' Laura closed the
book after committing the page number to memory
and placed it on the table. 'Is there anything else I can
do for you, Mrs Hunter?'

'Yes, dear. Tell Annie I want to speak to her.'

Some minutes later, mission completed, Laura
joined Blaise Hunter in his study.

'Did you want to see that movie?' he asked. Judith
and Steven were watching *Death on the Nile* in the
projection room.

'Not particularly. I can see it again.' She was so nervous she brushed against a cabinet and a file, loaded
with papers, clattered to the floor. She had made a
desperate little effort to save it, but still he clicked his
tongue and swept her aside.

'I'd be very grateful to you, Miss Mallory, if you
would *sit down*.'

Oh, you beast! she thought wretchedly, and carried
herself safely to a chair.

Instead of stepping back behind his desk, he sat on
the edge of it facing her. 'I've some news for you,' he
said.

'Of what?'

'I'm going to shock you,' he told her bluntly.

'You always do.' She looked up at him almost helplessly, acutely sensitive to his dark, frightening attrac-
tion.

'But do you trust me?'

'I. . . .'

'Look at me.'

'Yes, I do.' She lifted her head to meet his eyes.

'That much we're sure of.' He looked at her

sombrely. 'You never actually gave me permission, but when you first came here you were deeply unhappy, so unhappy you just didn't care about demanding anything for yourself, which is what Howard tried to get you to do.'

'And?'

'I know *you*. I've met your stepmother and I came to feel something could be wrong with your father's will. Little things your stepmother said added to Howard's being very vocal on the subject.'

'So what did you do?' Laura was so agitated, she sprang up, and incredibly Blaise put his two hands to her narrow waist and held her still.

'Well, to begin with, I had everyone take a closer look at that will.'

'Only I didn't *tell* you to!'

'Only I couldn't take you very seriously. You're little more than a child, an innocent, and you were undoubtedly in shock.'

She put up a hand and brushed it against her forehead. 'Are you going to tell me something horrible?'

'Something much worse. Two handwriting experts have considerable doubt it's your father's signature at all, and his partner has expressed the opinion that it would never happen, your being left out of your father's will. In fact, he was dumbfounded when he was told. As were a lot of people when the news leaked out.'

'I'm sorry. . . .' Laura swayed a little and he tightened his hands. 'Are you trying to tell me somebody forged it?'

'I'm telling you there is that distinct possibility.'

'But that's criminal!'

'I know.'

'But Jamie? It's Jamie I'm worried about!' Her voice

seemed to be coming with a great effort.

'Jamie was amply provided for in the earlier will which is in Howard's possession. As were you.'

Laura closed her eyes then and dropped her blonde head. 'It can't be right,' she whispered.

'What do you want to do?'

'Nothing.'

'You're whispering.' He caught hold of her chin and lifted her face to him. 'Laura, what do you want *me* to do?'

After weeks of 'Miss Mallory', the 'Laura' was a violent pleasure, so much so she felt too fragile to stand.

Blaise must have noted it in her sudden pallor, for he lowered her back into the chair. 'Sit down.' He stood silently looking at her.

'I feel strange,' she muttered.

'You obviously need looking after.' He turned and walked away to a wall cabinet that housed a collection of drinks and when he turned back he had a tumbler in his hand. 'Here, drink it. It won't hurt you and it might get you to talk.'

She sipped it, found the brandy fiery, at the same time calming the sinking sensation in her stomach. 'Are you paying people to investigate this?' she asked.

'No one works for nothing,' he returned brusquely. 'Do you find it hard to accept that the will could be a forgery?'

'But that would involve other people!' she exclaimed. 'Paula might do it, but how would she get witnesses who would be prepared to sign such a document?'

'I believe they're close friends of hers,' he pointed out, with no trace of pity for any of them. 'Men and women are in the courts every day for criminal deception, and nearly always it involves big sums of money.

Your stepmother could have been prepared to go to any lengths to secure everything for herself and for her son. It's been done before today.'

'And that's *it*, isn't it?' she said with a bewildered little laugh. 'Paula is Jamie's mother. If I hurt Paula I hurt my little brother, and I can't do that. His happiness is more important to me than getting my share of the money. Why, how could I let it be known his mother is a common criminal?'

'I was thinking of another way,' said Blaise.

'I don't think I want to know.'

'Shut up! Your selflessness is incredible. And you don't understand the situation. Obviously we can't fight this in the courts, but when your stepmother realises the terrible trouble she's in, I think she'll accept whatever proposition we put to her.'

'I only want her to let me see Jamie!'

'And you won't, not ever again, if you don't listen to me.' Blaise spoke rapidly, forcefully, very sure of himself, and because there was nothing else to do, Laura swallowed the rest of the strength-giving brandy. 'If we're right and I have more than my own hunch and all your good friends' opinions to go on, we won't have any trouble with your stepmother.'

'I don't want to punish her,' Laura said, and shuddered, as much in reaction as the effects of the brandy. 'I don't know that I even believe she could do something so terrible.'

'Don't forget, Miss Mallory,' he drawled sardonically, 'you're an angel!'

Her slender body, sheathed in a gold-threaded brown and black sundress with a camisole top, was no longer rigid with shock. She leaned back in the big burgundy leather chair, tilted her head sideways and closed her eyes. 'I do think sometimes it's a terrible life,' she muttered.

'Exactly my own viewpoint,' he said with a wry humour. 'You're very susceptible to brandy.'

'Nonsense!' She opened her eyes, her luminous glance entangling with his own.

'Try standing up.'

She shrugged, trying to overcome the sweet lassitude in her body. 'Of course I can.'

'I want to see you.'

'Look here, you gave it to me,' Laura protested.

'I was concerned,' he told her.

She didn't know exactly how it happened, but she gave him her hands. 'Help me.'

'What have you got in mind?' Blaise asked.

'*What?*' She jerked her head back and her thick, silky hair moved back in a wave.

'I can see through you, Miss Mallory,' he said, brilliant mockery in his eyes.

'You overrate yourself.'

'I'm only facing facts.'

She was on her feet now and he was sitting on the desk staring at her in such a way she felt under attack. 'The fact is, I work for you and I'm in no danger of forgetting it.'

'I wish I could say the same!'

He could hardly mean what she thought he meant, but still the telltale colour quickened under her creamy skin.

'I know you've had your successes with governesses in the past,' she burst out unguardedly.

'Why, you impertinent little bitch!'

She saw his face tauten, giving fair warning, and she stumbled in her haste to back away from him.

'Explain that, won't you?' he said silkily, coming after her.

'I beg your pardon. I was very rude.'

Blaise nodded, his eyes like black diamonds. 'What do you take me for, anyway? A seducer of dim-witted girls?'

'I said I was sorry.'

Now he had grasped her arms. 'Too easy, your apology!'

'You *can't* think a thrashing would be more fitting?'

'Why not something worse?' she retorted. 'You can file it under a big E for Experience.'

'Please don't,' she begged him. 'It would be something far too powerful for me.'

'*Don't.*' He mimicked her tone, his hand against the softness of her skin. '*Do*, you mean. *I* know it. *You* know it. The problem is, how to hide from it.' His thumb stroked her cheekbone, tracing the line. 'What did you feel when we met, Miss Mallory?'

Laura thought she shivered. She wasn't sure.

'You've been afraid of this, haven't you?'

'Of course. Yes.' She couldn't take her eyes off him.

'And you're so right.' He moved aside her heavy hair, bent his head and kissed the satin skin of her neck, and as she shuddered convulsively put his arms around her and locked her to him, her breasts against his hard chest, slender hips, long legs, the length of her body pressed against his.

All the strength ran out of her, the excitement was so enormous. She heard herself gasp in involuntary pleasure, saw his narrowing, brilliant black eyes, then the warm shape of his mouth covering her own, so ravishing at the first contact she opened her own mouth immediately, consciously inviting the deeper exploration he demanded. . . .

She wanted him at that moment more than she had ever wanted anything else in her whole life—strong

arms encircling her, crushing her, his mouth feeding
on her own, the wanting so intense it was draining her
of all her precious energy, putting her body under
stress. His own hunger seemed insatiable, more violent
than voluptuous, sensations coming so rapidly it was
like being lifted by a giant wave.

'*Blaise!*' She thought she moaned his name aloud in
anguish, either against the wave or her own tumultuous
emotions, then he was lifting her, just as swiftly to
put her down so her torso twisted back against the
deep leather sofa, the studs pressing into her bare
skin.

'I tell you, you're fainting!'

'Who's fainting?' There was a jewelled field before
her eyes, diamonds and rubies and sapphires. She had
to blink hard.

'I think *you* were.' Blaise's voice sounded oddly
urgent.

'*Me?*' Her ash-blonde head fell back and he swung
her legs up on to the sofa. 'Why should you expect me
to faint at a little excitement.'

'Laura?' His voice sounded serious.

'I'm all right.' She closed her eyes.

'You're a baby.'

'Oh, that sounded tender!'

'Come on,' he took her hands and held them, 'you
know I'm not capable of that sort of thing.'

'Well, at least you won't try kissing me again.'

'Lie still for a moment,' he ordered.

'I tell you I'm all right,' Laura protested. 'I just felt
weak for a moment. It was as if I let you own me.'

'Obviously you've never felt like it before.'

'Isn't that ridiculous?'

'It's interesting.' His dark voice had an edge of
amusement. 'Open your eyes.'

'As you wish.' Her grey eyes were enormous and her skin was very pale.

'Better?' he asked, still with that half-tender impatience.

'Yes, my heart has stopped fluttering.'

'Has it?' His black eyes moved from her face to the creamy curve of her breast, faintly bitter now.

'Don't look like that,' she said quickly, lifting her body up, though he kept her legs trapped.

'Oh?' Blaise's mouth twisted sardonically, 'like what, Laura?'

'Bitter.'

'Absolutely.'

'It's a bad idea to dwell on the past.'

'I've read all that too.' His glance was very cool now, that of a stranger.

'Forgive me,' she said. 'I have no right to say anything.'

'No, Miss Mallory, you haven't.'

'And you have no right to kiss me,' she added indignantly, alienated by his arrogance.

'Well, think again, my pure beauty.' He locked his two hands beneath her rib cage. 'I want you, as much as you want me, though none of this was any of our idea. In fact, if you weren't a little virgin, I'd have you tonight.'

'Allowing, of course, plenty of time to knock me unconscious.'

He gave a brief, amused laugh. 'I think I could spare you that little tribal custom.'

'I really should go,' she said, and her voice was shaky and low.

'I quite believe you.'

'Then let me up.'

'You've only just told me you wanted to go.' Blaise

looked so careless and mocking she gave a little muffled exclamation.

'*Please*, Blaise!'

'Mr Hunter, to you,' he goaded her.

'Mr Hunter, then.'

'Mm.' He suddenly caught her chin and the tears swam into her eyes.

'You're a brute and a bully!'

'Save that for the time I decide to abduct you.'

Laura hesitated unhappily, but he had obviously decided to bring things back to normal. 'Up with you!' he lifted her like a feather, eyeing her sardonically as she fussed with the crushed skirt of her dress. 'Don't worry, Miss Mallory, you look very charming.'

'I have a positive horror of. . . .'

'Lovemaking?'

His slow, mocking drawl was infuriating. 'I was going to say . . . oh, it's hardly worth while.' She lifted her flushed face, her thick blonde hair tumbling, and he lifted his winged eyebrows.

'And to make matters worse, you *look* as if you've been through something fairly torrid,' he told her.

'Then isn't it a good thing Claudia isn't here?' she said sweetly.

'Claudia?' he gave an indolent shrug. 'Claudia, my dear, has never turned me on.'

'No, but she has the advantage of not being a virgin.'

'You don't *mean* it?'

Laura was ashamed of herself as soon as she had said it, but all the smooth mockery had distracted her. 'I'm sorry for that,' she apologised immediately.

'I should hope so! Little Miss Angelica being bitchy.'

'Let's say we're both at fault.'

'Be honest, Miss Mallory, you've been trying to get me to kiss you for weeks.'

'I deny it.' She walked away quickly to the door.

'I'm surprised you would want to,' Blaise commented.

'Oh, heavens!' She shook her head helplessly, and when she looked up he was studying her with a strange expression on his face, a hint of the indulgence he showed Liza. 'By the way,' she said shakily, 'thank you for getting the pony in for Liza. I'm sure I'm going to be able to teach her.'

'You *will*.' Now the dark, brooding look was back on his face again. 'I'm as certain of that as I am of anything. You're very good for her.'

'Thank you.' She was still slightly out of breath.

'We must call you Golden Lotus, weaving spells everywhere.'

Laura turned sharply at his tone, but his question drew her back. 'Do you trust me to save your inheritance?'

'You seem certain you can.' He loomed tall and strikingly handsome behind her.

'It may necessitate a meeting with your stepmother, then a fairly rapid dénouement.'

'There can't be any charges,' Laura insisted.

'I know that.' He searched her wide, silver-grey eyes. 'You have no taste for vengeance, have you?'

'None at all.'

'Maybe that's what makes you so fascinating!' His tone was very clinical and detached. 'A girl who would seem to be as good as she's beautiful. Goodnight, Miss Mallory. Leave everything to me.'

The following morning saw the first of Liza's riding lessons, but she had been so psyched up on myth and legend she was almost mad to take off.

'It went well, don't you think?' Laura asked her after the adorable little Honey had been turned out into a paddock.

'I should be able to gallop on my own tomorrow.' Sturdy little Liza, once described by Claudia as pathologically afraid of horses, was now the assured horse-woman.

'Well, not quite tomorrow, dear, but you can see it's going to be fun.'

'And Blaise got Honey especially for *me*.' Liza was still bowled over by her entrancing present.

'And you named her.'

'Oh, that part was easy. She is a honey,' Liza laughed. 'Maybe Blaise will let me go along on the bullock muster. Gosh, the hill country is rough, but there's a lot of good dry feed. I've seen it from the helicopter, the great spread of spinifex. It would be grand chasing all those wild-eyed cattle! They feed in mobs, but when they see a horseman coming they break up, pounding off in all directions. No two of them seem to stay together, and the area they can stray off into is *immense*.'

'Which would make the use of the helicopter easy to understand.'

'That's right!' Liza all but tumbled over a large stone that bordered the jungly part of the garden with its strong, tropical foliage forms. 'Heck,' she muttered, angry with herself for falling over the everyday trap, 'wouldn't you think someone would shift that?'

'Why don't we?' Laura bent down quietly and rolled the large stone back into the garden, and as she did so, a long green snake flagrantly slithered out in front of her. 'Oh, no!' she recoiled in horror.

'It won't hurt you,' Liza told her complacently. 'Gosh, we've got *real* snakes here—killers.'

'I don't want to see them.' Laura could feel herself distinctly shaking.

'You want to see the olive pythons after a heavy meal! They look so funny. But I guess what would really frighten you would be the goannas. Some of them are six feet long and when they stand up they look like dinosaurs. Did you know one of them tried to run up a stockman and he nearly died of a heart attack? And others have been known to run at the horses. We've got wild camels too, they're pretty fierce, and we're always trying to keep down the dingoes.'

'Quite a zoo!' said Laura dryly.

'The dingoes attack the young calves, didn't you know?'

'Yes, I did.' Laura moved quite a few feet from the garden, flapping her feet as though a snake might be under them.

'Yes, a big problem, dingoes,' Liza continued like a dwarf professor, 'yet they look super when they're in prime condition. We were camped in the desert once and a big dingo came in and made off with Ted's socks. A lot of them have never seen a human being. Blaise tells me they can be very tame, but they're really killers by nature, you know. When you hear a howling dingo, you'll know. It's a terribly creepy sound.'

They were almost back at the homestead, and Laura looked up as she always did at the beautiful Georgian house. It was really so majestic, yet welcoming, as one immediately recognised it was the centre of a family and a long family tradition. She particularly loved the portico with its Corinthian columns, in fact she loved classical columns altogether.

'What's Sean doing here?' Liza asked.

The overseer was moving up the wide flight of steps, but when he saw Laura he turned around, doffing his dusty, wide-brimmed Stetson rather selfconsciously.

''Morning, Miss Mallory—Liza.'

'Good morning.' Laura looked at him and smiled, but Sean's normally goodnatured expression was overlaid with definite anxiety. 'Something wrong?'

'The Boss up at the house?' Sean asked.

'Uncle Steven is.' Liza supplied.

'It's the Boss I'm after.'

'I haven't seen him,' said Laura, suddenly realising most people bypassed Steven for his brother without a trace of hesitation.

'I've got to find him,' Sean announced. 'There's been trouble.'

'What trouble?' Liza had completely lost her beaming smile.

'Hell,' Sean didn't answer, looking desperate, and just at that moment a jeep tore up the long, empty drive towards them. 'I hope that's him now!'

Blaise parked a few feet away from them and got out. 'What the hell is this I hear?' he demanded, his anger controlled, but radiating out towards them so that it almost broke against their bodies.

'A dozen bullocks,' said Sean, looking as if he was about to buckle at the knees. 'I won't try to tell you how wild I am, Boss. You know it.'

'The vicious bastard!' Pinpoints of light were flaring in Blaise's black eyes and he looked someone quite different from all the other Blaises Laura had seen before. He looked frightening—the cattle baron, the real thing.

'He won't get far,' Sean muttered, rocking a little on his tall heels.

'That's right, he won't, the son of a bitch!' Blaise said explosively. 'I know every damned inch of this country.'

'He's got a gun and a four-wheel-drive.'

'Nothing will protect him.' For the first time Blaise seemed to notice the girls, both standing looking up at him with ill-concealed bewilderment and a kind of female intimidation. A man's world was a tough one, but most of the time the harshness was concealed from them. Now those brilliant black eyes that could be filled with amusement or mockery were burning coldly with no trace of softness at all. He looked the abstraction of anger made visible, a granite-hard man.

'Go into the house and get Steven,' he told Liza sharply. 'Tell him I want him *right now*.'

'Sure, Blaise!' Liza rushed forward to obey him.

'What's wrong?' Laura heard herself asking anxiously, unconsciously bracing herself as he looked at her directly.

'Twelve prime beasts,' he told her. 'Slaughtered, just like that. A vicious, cowardly act to get square with me. Benson, the man I put off.'

'I should never have hired him, Boss,' Sean said unhappily, 'but he seemed a big, enduring sort of bloke.'

'And brutal,' Blaise said curtly. 'I told you that. Anyway, we're bound to get a bad one from time to time. The thing to do now is get him and deal with him.'

'How?' Laura was getting terrible visions of a lynching.

'Fair and square,' he said shortly, 'so don't go getting big-eyed.'

Steven came running as most people did, and a few minutes later, all three men left in the jeep.

'I wonder what they're going to do?' Liza asked of Mrs Madden as they sat around the kitchen. 'Sean said Benson had a gun.'

'Mr Hunter will take care of it,' Mrs Madden tossed cabbage into the shredder. 'He'll probably get in a few thumps into the bargain. I'm amazed anyone chose to make trouble.'

'He got kicked out,' Liza told her.

'He'll get knocked out when they catch up with him,' Mrs Madden exclaimed with a grimace. 'I tell you, my dears, I wouldn't like to be in that man's shoes!'

The rest of the day couldn't be normal, but when Steven finally came back to the house just on sunset he told them offhandedly that 'the wretched Benson' had been delivered to Sergeant Norman where he could 'make a recovery' in jail.

'Gosh,' said Liza, 'I suppose we wouldn't recognise him.'

During the next few days with the bullock muster set in action they saw very little of the men at all, but at the weekend, several members of a buying syndicate, along with their wives, flew in on a combined business and pleasure trip.

Laura stood by her window watching them arrive. The men looked very large and prosperous, one of them ludicrously bow-legged, and the women were dressed very expensively, absorbing their fabulous surroundings with a mixture of envy and eye-popping delight. Everyone knew the Hunters had made their fortune, but did they have to live in a Greek temple?

Liza walked over to her, almost knocking a small bronze statue off its stand, and slid her hand into Laura's. 'I hate it when we have visitors,' she confided.

'Why, dear?' Laura stepped back to look down at her.

'I wish they wouldn't stare at me all the time.'

'Why ever do you think that?'

'Because, you see, they *do*.' Liza pulled Laura forward so they could both drop down on the side of the bed. 'Will you think less of me, Laura, if I tell you a secret?'

'I couldn't think less of you for *anything*!' Laura turned on the child the calmest, kindest face in the world.

'You see,' Liza told her, 'it's really something unusual, something you'll never expect.'

'Tell me.'

Liza moved closer to the comfort of Laura's body. 'I haven't told anyone else, but I don't mind if you know. You see, I'm Blaise's adopted daughter.'

'Liza,' Laura said very simply and solemnly. How did the child know?

'There, I knew you'd be surprised! Of course, Blaise loves me like his real daughter. He's told me I'm his little pal and no one is ever going to take me from him, *ever*.'

'Of course not.'

'But he didn't have the great honour of being my father. My real father is dead, and Blaise told me he accepted me as his very own.'

'And when was this?' Laura asked, her grey eyes wide.

'Oh, ages ago,' Liza said peacefully. 'Blaise and I had quite a chat in his study. He told me he thought I was mature enough to handle the truth. He's very complimentary, Blaise.'

'And you *are* mature, Liza,' Laura said faintly.

'Of course I was terribly surprised at the time, but Blaise swore it made no difference to him, so it makes no difference to me. He said he was very proud of me—and you know, Blaise expects a lot.'

'He does indeed,' Laura seconded vaguely. 'And you

haven't told anyone else?'

'Blaise says who needs to know but him and me. But people are very curious. I expect it's because I don't look like Blaise.'

'You have a way of him,' Laura said. 'I suppose it's his strong fatherly influence.'

'Yes, exactly,' said Liza, in a pleased voice. 'Blaise said my name is Liza Hunter, I'm his daughter and that's settled.'

'Thank you for telling me, Liza,' Laura said gently.

'I thought it was proper seeing we're such good friends.' Liza seemed relieved to have the whole thing off her mind.

'And it hasn't changed things at all. You're still the same Liza.'

'The only thing that bothers me I would have *looked* nicer, if Blaise had been my other father. He's so handsome, isn't he?' Liza looked up at her, one woman to the other.

'Stunning.' It would have been absurd to deny it.

'To tell you the truth,' Liza conceded, 'I wouldn't mind if Blaise married you, but when I told him it seemed to strike him as very funny.'

'You *told* him?' Laura faltered.

'Oh, he wasn't angry, but he thinks you're a sort of schoolgirl. You know what I mean.'

'Glory!'

'Anyway,' said Liza, 'don't worry. We both know you're not.'

CHAPTER SEVEN

IT had been decided on that fine evening to dine out of doors, a very lavish barbecue their sophisticated visitors found wonderfully relaxing. The huge verandah that projected from the rear façade was perfect for dancing and in the centre of the great open-air court was a swimming pool that glowed peacock blue at night.

'Oh, this is such an experience!' Olivia Harrison, one of the wives, crooned extravagantly. A handsome, over-ripe brunette, she had spent most of her time following Blaise with her eyes. 'I think I shall swim later when all this wonderful food has gone down.'

She hadn't missed lunch either, Laura recalled, wishing for the hundredth time she had been excused from the gathering. Obviously the women were going to ignore her and the bow-legged buyer with the ridiculous big moustache was going to keep leering at her like some half-witted hyena.

'What's wrong with you?' Judith asked in passing. 'You're very quiet.'

'I don't think you understand,' Laura said wryly, 'I'm the governess.'

'The governess?' Judith looked back at her in blank astonishment, then burst out laughing. 'Oh, the governess. Oh, I *see*.' Three of the four ladies had given the marked impression that staff should be isolated from guests and the other, a rather frigid thin woman, had never taken her eyes off her. Finally, the thin lady sauntered over.

'Good evening,' she said, unimaginatively.

'Mrs Landers.' Laura had only then recalled the woman's name.

'I hear you're the new governess?'

She had certainly been introduced as Liza's governess. 'Yes,' Laura smiled politely.

'And how are you finding the job?'

'Not a job at all, a pleasure.'

'Is that so?' Mrs Landers raised her thin brows and looked down her sharp nose. 'You look a very unlikely choice, if you don't mind my saying so.'

'Why is that?' Laura returned brightly.

'You're rather amazingly good-looking, for one thing. I couldn't have been more surprised.'

Or more disapproving, Laura thought.

'You are a *trained* governess?' Mrs Landers asked.

'Do you mean do I have the necessary qualifications to teach an eight-year-old?' Laura asked.

'I believe she took no notice at all of the other two.'

'Someone told you?'

'My dear, people talk for all they're worth.'

'And I expect a lot of the talk is worthless. I really do.'

'I see.' A spiteful look crossed Mrs Landers' face. 'I expect *you* wouldn't be here, unless you were told things.'

'I'm not with you, Mrs Landers,' Laura said.

'Well, I think you are. A young girl cooped up in the wilds—what girl would want that unless she knew what sort of a place she was going to, what sort of people. I don't see why we shouldn't mention that Blaise Hunter is one of the most eligible men around, and *so* handsome, for all that poor plain child looks like nobody.'

'You should tell him that,' Laura said challengingly.

'Say in front of him what you're saying behind his back.'

Mrs Landers smiled thinly. 'My dear, I'm not a fool. It's a way of life, talking about rich people. Especially when there's so much to say.'

'You must know a lot of nosey parkers,' Laura said bluntly, disgusted that the woman could accept so much lavish hospitality and repay it with malicious innuendo.

'My, you're certainly an aggressive girl, aren't you?' Mrs Landers emphasised. 'But never mind. Young girls are these days, even if they still believe in the old Cinderella story—you know, the one where the poor little nobody meets the handsome prince and marries him. A sweet story, but oh, so improbable!'

'Nevertheless it does happen,' Laura said composedly, though her hands were faintly trembling as they did when she was upset. 'Would you excuse me, Mrs Landers? I think I'll be happier elsewhere.'

To say Mrs Landers was incensed was putting it mildly, and Laura didn't think it would take her long to complain about the governess's extraordinary lack of manners. In any case, Mrs Landers' prince was a toad. Leering, it seemed, wasn't enough for him, and as the evening wore on he made his ungainly way to Laura's side, his hooded eyes running the length of her in what Laura could only think of as a lascivious fashion.

'You don't do shorthand and typing, do you, young lady?'

'I'm afraid not.' She could type, of course, and quite well.

'I have a few letters I'd like to get off.'

'I daresay someone from the office could help you,' she said politely.

'Are they as pretty as you?' He slumped into the tobacco brown wicker chair with its plush white upholstery.

'The emphasis is on efficiency,' she said lightly. 'I believe Arthur does the typing.'

'In that case, never mind.' A hint of hostility flashed out from the cosy bonhomie. Like his wife, Mr Landers could become very unpleasant if anyone crossed him.

'What were you and my wife babbling about?' he asked her.

'Just social pleasantries, Mr Landers.'

'You're an uncommunicative girl, aren't you?' he said in a patronising tone. 'This your first job?'

'Yes, it is.'

'Kind of unusual, isn't it?'

'In what way?'

'Girlie,' he laughed jeeringly, 'with your looks you could be famous, get into modelling or something like that.'

'I'm afraid that wouldn't appeal to me, Mr Landers.' Laura stood up with a pretence at casualness.

'Say, don't run away.' His fingers exerted considerable pressure against her wrist and just as Laura was contemplating a scene, Blaise Hunter excused himself from his more civilised guests and came towards them, looking big and powerful and magnificently fastidious.

'If I didn't know you were a gentleman, Ray, I might think you were trying to detain Miss Mallory against her will!'

'Good gosh, no!' Over Ray Landers' face spread a look of incredulity and dismay. 'Miss Mallory and I were having a nice little talk.'

'Then it seems a pity to break it up, but that's what I'm going to do.'

'Hey now, Blaise!' Ray Landers stood up quickly, forcing a laugh. 'Surely I haven't annoyed you?'

'A misunderstanding, I'm sure.' He spoke quietly, smoothly, but it compelled Ray Landers to look at Laura with an air of helpless apology.

'Tell your boss here I haven't said one word to offend you.'

'Of course not!' Laura complied instantly, realising as the detestable Mr Landers did that there was a kind of menace behind Blaise Hunter's suave manner. 'I merely decided to say an early goodnight. I have an assignment to catch up on.'

'Go on!' Ray Landers spoke in a more normal tone. 'It doesn't sound like a lot of fun.'

'Would you excuse me, Mr Hunter?' Laura asked politely, painfully aware of his air of formidability.

'Certainly.' He barely glanced at her. 'Don't worry about saying goodnight to the others, I'll say it for you.'

It was clearly a dismissal and Laura made her way inside inwardly wincing. It was a shock—Ray Landers' crudity, his wife's malice, but she recognised the pain came from Blaise Hunter's faintly contemptuous attitude. Surely he didn't think she had given the ghastly Mr Landers the faintest encouragement to grasp her arm? Judith had told her the Landers were new names to the syndicate, but that Ray Landers, some kind of entrepreneur, was 'rotten with money'. He had rotten manners as well. She couldn't even bear to think about the horrible insolence of his open stare. It was a nasty experience to have been touched by him.

When she entered her room, she leant back against the door, catching her reflection in the full-length Victorian mirror tilting on its stand. Her dress was very pretty and partified, in a rich cardinal red with a low neck, puffed sleeves and a gleaming gold sash-belt at her enviably small waist. Her evening sandals were gold too, as were her leaf-shaped earrings, but her appearance, which had originally pleased her, had only added another dimension to the evening and one they could well have done without. It was not necessary to make friends of the people one did business with, on the other hand one didn't seek to antagonise them either. Blaise Hunter had given the decided impression that one more impertinence from Mr Landers and he could consider himself out of the running. Yet he had done nothing all that spectacular. A lot of men directed glances at women that could be considered offensive, but if everything else was correct, it had to be tolerated. Of course he *had* caught her wrist, but she had tried to keep her face courteously blank. Nevertheless Blaise Hunter had come over to them, his manner, behind the deliberate suaveness, ominous enough to force an apology of sorts from his guest. The thought made Laura anxious and she wondered if at some time she might be blamed for it.

For the rest of their visitors' stay, she kept well out of the way. The swimming pool was much in use, so she and Liza sought the secluded peace of Paradise Pool, which was much what they preferred anyway.

'Who's that man that keeps staring at you?' Liza asked her, so adult in her observations she often took Laura by surprise.

'A Mr Landers,' Laura answered in some surprise.

'He's more like a bullfrog,' Liza said primly. 'And have you ever seen a sillier moustache? I just wish they'd go.'

'So do I.' It was true two of the buyers had turned out to be quite pleasant, even more the voluptuous Mrs Harrison had had a small conversation with Laura and

appeared to hang on every word, but the Landers'
presence was straining the atmosphere. Whether he
was conscious of it or not Ray Landers was displaying
an embarrassing interest in catching sight of Laura,
and she could only attribute this to an apparent fixation
on blondes.

Even pre-warned, Laura was dismayed to see him
approaching them as she and Liza returned from their
swim.

'Oh, heck, it's the bullfrog!' Liza hissed, catching
Laura's sudden tension.

' 'Afternoon, girls!' Ray Landers roared amiably, his
curiously hooded eyes registering the same preoc-
cupation with Laura's face and form, all the more so
because, approaching the house by a side door, she
had merely draped her brilliantly coloured beach
sarong around her like a skirt and her upper body in
its black swimsuit gleamed a light honey gold.

Neither girl smiled, but Liza said politely: 'Hello,
Mr Landers.'

He gave her a brief stare and the hooded eyes
rounded. 'Been swimming, have you?'

'That's right.' Laura's hand tightened on the little
girl's, but Liza was already moving willingly. 'And
we're very untidy. Would you excuse us, Mr
Landers?'

'Gracious, you needn't race off every time you see
me!' He gave her the approximation of a conciliatory
smile, but the edge was in his voice. 'Anyone would
think you didn't trust me.'

'Not at all,' Laura told him, 'but as you can see, we
need to change.'

'Not *you*, girl,' he said with great heartiness. 'You
look just beautiful.'

'Why are you bothering Laura?' Liza suddenly burst

out, and Ray Landers glared at her.

'Oh, that's too bad, little lady. Why don't you run off and let the adults talk?'

The effect on Liza wasn't at all what Laura expected, for her staunch little friend broke away from her abruptly and raced down the deserted path.

'Best move she could have made,' Ray Landers observed tightly. 'Unpleasant little kid, and as plain as the devil. Extraordinary, don't you think, when the Hunters were such a lovely couple.'

Laura went to step past him, but he put out his arm. 'Say, hold it, blondie. What have you got to be so much up in the air about? Why do you give yourself more airs and graces than an actual member of the family?'

'Please take your hand from my shoulder,' she said, her face registering her extreme distaste.

'You don't really mean it, do you?' His eyes flicked from her ash-blonde hair to her mouth to the cleft between her breasts. 'I could do a lot for you, blondie. Lots of things happen for pretty girls. Give up your job here and you could count on me to help you. All you have to do is say the word.'

'And the word is—*move!*' Laura snapped.

'Nonsense. I fancy you.'

'And I find you extremely offensive.'

'What a shame!' The big, calloused hand shaped her shoulder. 'I guess you're keeping yourself for Hunter, are you?'

Laura was so angry she nearly choked. 'Instead of saying such things to me, why don't you say them to Mr Hunter? If you're game!'

'Who the hell is he anyway?' Ray Landers jerked her towards him, power in his ungainly body. 'So he's got money! So have I. Plenty to buy *you* a few lovely surprises. What sort of money would a little governess make? Laughable, a few dollars. I guess Hunter's the big cattle baron with a fine background and a big castle, but he's had his share of trouble, count on it. He's only amusing himself with you.'

'You're disgusting!'

'And you're tantalising.' The big, sensual mouth curled up and he slipped his fingers beneath the thin strap of her swimsuit and pushed it off her shoulder. 'Such skin!'

Before Laura could even hit out, a woman's piercing voice shrieked from behind them. 'Ray!'

It was Mrs Landers, and her sharp features were arranged in an expression of utter outrage. 'If Mr Hunter had any sense,' she told Laura venomously, 'he'd send you packing!'

'Then I'd suggest he put us all on the same plane.' Laura adjusted her swimsuit, her voice cool but her hand trembling. 'You must have discovered by now that your husband is a lecher.'

'Cut it out, sweetie,' Ray Landers was openly laughing. 'You know you were giving me the great big come-on.'

'I'm going to make it my business to see Mr Hunter knows,' Mrs Landers cried shrilly. 'As the wife of a rich man I've had to accept the fact that girls fling themselves at my husband.'

'I'd say they were more likely to jump off a building, but if fantasies make you happy. . . .'

'How dare you, you insolent girl!' Mrs Landers angled her hand as if to slap Laura's face, but Blaise Hunter's ringing tone made them all jump.

'What the devil goes on here?' He was much taller than Ray Landers, much taller than any of them, and he had moved up on them swiftly with his peculiarly silent, cat-like tread.

Ray Landers ran his hand over his suddenly florid cheeks. 'Why, nothin', Blaise. A purely friendly little discussion.'

'I didn't see your wife about to strike Miss Mallory?'

'For cryin' out loud!' Ray Landers laughed genially, 'I expect you saw her tryin' to swat an insect.' He turned and gave his wife a bright, dangerous look. 'Isn't that right, May?'

'You're only trying to protect the girl,' his wife returned coldly, 'but the fact is, Mr Hunter, this young woman has been trying to attract my husband's attention almost from the moment we arrived. You may have noticed it yourself, it's been so obvious.'

Blaise Hunter eyed her coolly, his arrogant head up. 'You show considerable loyalty, Mrs Landers, the way you put it, but when you're dealing with me and my staff, I should like you to stick to the truth.'

'Oh. . . .' Mrs Landers' vehement expression wavered oddly, and she looked to her husband for support.

'We don't need you any more, Miss Mallory.' Blaise Hunter's black gaze whipped over Laura with a cold and certain anger.

She turned away and walked the little distance up the side path to the side door. 'Laura!' Liza was calling to her, her round face a study. 'I can't move. I've strained every muscle in my body.'

'How?' Laura looked up sharply and ran up the stairs to where Liza was sitting in a peculiarly slumped fashion.

'Did you find it very awful?' Liza asked. 'I ran nearly the whole length of the compound trying to find Blaise.'

'Oh, Liza!' Laura slumped down beside her, feeling

such a wave of affection she hugged the child. 'Was it you?'

'Of course it was!' Liza was discovering she was feeling better. 'You didn't think I was going to leave you there with that nasty man?'

'I might have known you wouldn't.' Laura repressed a shudder. 'I'm afraid your father is very angry.'

'I expect the Landers will leave now.' Liza's tone was casual. 'Blaise said you being what you are we can't avoid trouble.'

'And what *am* I?' Laura shook her head blankly.

'Don't worry. I'm sure he means you're lovely.'

Despite Liza's reassurances, Laura felt distracted for the rest of the day, and old Mrs Hunter, even with her failing eyesight, was perceptive enough to notice Laura's hidden agitation.

'Is there something bothering you, my dear?' she asked, her assured voice gentle with understanding.

Unconsciously Laura picked up the silver-framed photograph of Blaise Hunter as a handsome, confident twelve-year-old and clutched it to her. 'You'll probably hear in any case, but I'm afraid I've attracted a good deal of unwanted attention from one of Mr Hunter's guests.'

Old Mrs Hunter inclined her snow-white head. 'That Landers person?'

'Have you heard?' Laura's delicate arched eyebrows rose in surprise.

'Blaise said one or two words.'

'I don't think he liked or approved of the whole situation.' Laura still stood with the photograph pressed to her. 'I just hope he doesn't blame me. You see, things came to a climax this afternoon and I was told not to appear at dinner.'

'Blaise would only wish to spare you any more annoyance.' Mrs Hunter's voice was soft and almost amused. 'You're worrying about nothing, my dear girl. Now, put that photograph down, though you're free to look at it whenever you like, and we'll speak about more pleasant things—the support you are to me and the fine job you're doing with Liza. Incidentally,' she put out her hand and caught Laura's fingertips, 'Steven told me you and he had a talk about little Liza. I tried once to tell you, but you see, I've always found the subject so terribly upsetting, as if I were as helpless now as I was then. Faced with a harsh fact none of us could alter. I regard Liza with affection, you know that, but I'm only human. That child was the way Virginia chose to bring us down, to revenge herself against Blaise in the most dreadful way she could think of. I've never spoken about Virginia before and I won't now, except to say she was the most amoral person I have ever met. Yet even the way she was, Blaise did everything possible to help her, just as he has accepted Liza. God knows there has to come a time when he has to tell that child everything.' For a moment the old lady couldn't hide her distress, and Laura knelt down in front of her armchair and spoke carefully.

'Liza knows, Mrs Hunter. Your grandson told her in such a way that he saved almost all of their former relationship. Liza knows now he's not her real father but he has adopted her for his very own. She has accepted it in her own courageous little way, and best of all maintained her self-esteem. You see, Mr Hunter knew when to tell her, and he apparently told her in the best possible way. Things are near enough to being the same for Liza. She's the same privileged, sheltered, important little girl. Your grandson made that clear to her. She's someone special.'

Mrs Hunter sat numbly for a long time. '*Blaise* did?' she asked finally.

'Liza told me herself.'

'Dear Lord!' The old lady let her body relax against the high wingbacked chair. 'But then he's been making decisions a long time.'

'And he's awfully good at it.'

'Yes.' Mrs Hunter looked into the compassionate young face in front of her. 'The only mistake he ever made was Virginia, and it happens to all of us . . . some tragedy.'

'The tragedy is over,' Laura said anxiously, seeing the hurt in the still fine dark eyes.

'How?' the old lady asked wearily. 'Have you never wondered why he hasn't married again? Looking as he does, talking and acting the way he does. He's a powerful, prominent man, born to a splendid heritage, with no heir to take over. Steven doesn't want authority, you know. He has never really wanted our way of life, and he certainly won't want it for his children, when they come along. A man has to be cut out for a special destiny. Power might fall into a man's lap, but he won't be able to hold it unless he's strong and clever and determined. That's what makes the difference between my two grandsons. I love them both, but Blaise is different. Steven admits responsibility bothers him but Blaise shoulders it as though the weightiest decisions were cushions. He doesn't spare himself for Hunter's Moon, but sometimes I'm very much afraid there'll be no one of his calibre to come after him. Really, he *must* remarry, but I have to keep silent.' The great diamond on her hand flashed its blue light. 'I'm very tired tonight, Laura, I think I'll go to bed.'

'There must be something I can do for you.' Laura stood up quickly.

'I think I might have just a teeny brandy. It helps me to sleep.'

'Then I'll get it for you.'

'Thank you, dear.' The old lady's austere expression softened. 'And don't go worrying about Mr Landers. Blaise will deal with him.'

Downstairs Laura could hear laughter coming from the big, comfortably furnished room the family used for informal entertaining and showing movies, and Steven's voice issuing a challenge about who played the lead role in some vintage movie. Both Steven and Judith enjoyed company, Judith coming out of her rather brooding introspection to shine. Probably she too suffered from the immense isolation and the knowledge that her husband wasn't particularly happy in the role family responsibilities had cast him in.

To avoid being seen, she moved fleetingly down the passageway, when Blaise Hunter suddenly emerged from his study and stopped her.

'What do you want?' he asked sharply, his eyes lifting and going beyond her as though there could be a figure pursuing her.

'I'm getting something for your grandmother,' she said quickly, unnerved by his tone.

'Down here?' he challenged her crisply, the light behind the line of his powerful shoulders.

'Yes, here.' She reacted instinctively, tilting her chin. 'Your grandmother would like a small brandy to help her to sleep.'

'Is there something worrying her?' he asked, using one of his dominating gestures to indicate she was to precede him into the study.

'I think she's just a little tired.' She stood just inside the room, a slender figure in a summery white dress, waiting for him to say something hurtful. And he did.

'I don't expect to see you down here again tonight.'

'I don't *want* to come down here, Mr Hunter,' she said, and the quick colour flushed her skin. 'I want you to know that at no time did I give Mr Landers the slightest encouragement to single me out.'

'Let it go,' he said shortly. 'Though under the circumstances one could possibly have expected you to appear at all times properly dressed.'

He gave her a quite terrible gaze and she stared back at him, her throat dry. 'You mean you expected me to put a topcoat over my swimsuit?'

'At least it would have diverted Landers' attention,' he exploded. 'So you want to go swimming? *Go.* Just remember the ratio of men to women out here is about eighty to one, and you really give them something to look at.'

Clearly, the implication was, it was her fault. 'But how dreadfully unfair!' she exclaimed bitterly, a small pulse beginning to beat at the base of her throat.

'Unfair but true. You can't go wandering around like a little island of innocence when there's a big, bad man lurking behind every bush.'

'Are you trying to tell me,' she said heatedly, 'women have no choice?'

'I'm telling you, Miss Mallory,' he said flatly, 'they can't do as they damned well please—and please don't belabour me with sexual equality or whatever the hell else it is you have on your mind.'

At that moment she hated him, the appalling male arrogance. He had been determined from the moment he had met her to put her in the wrong and keep her there.

'May I have the brandy?' she said glacially.

'I'll take it.' His voice was now heavily spiced with sarcasm.

'Your grandmother expects *me*.' She was so angry she felt dizzy.

'Well, I'm cancelling the order.'

Laura actually had the impulse to hurl herself at him and hit him, some primitive scene where she could make her feelings perfectly clear.

'Goodnight, Miss Mallory.' He turned around and faced her directly, seeing the faint element of hysteria in her face.

'Goodnight, Mr Hunter.' She ground her small white teeth together. Every damn thing I get I asked for, she thought melodramatically.

'Don't go that way, go this.' Blaise walked to a side door that led through a progression of rooms to a rear stairway. And she knew why. He didn't want her to be seen. He wasn't looking after her, he was looking after his rich buyer.

Ordinarily she moved with a serene grace, now she wanted to fly to her room. She was so angry with him, with herself, it frightened her. Men—what arrogance! That was the worst of them. Forget the sexual hold they had on you. They would never liberate women at all.

It was her elbow that caught the glass and sent it crashing to the polished floor. Waterford crystal, not something cheap and replaceable.

'Oh, damn!' she cried moaningly, and dropped to her knees to pick the sparkling diamond-cut pieces up.

'Leave it,' he said with brittle impatience. 'Leave it, Laura, you'll cut yourself.'

'For heaven's sake, why worry?' Now she had tears in her eyes and she had no idea why. Why use the familiar, unnerving Laura once in a while? He was bending down to her and his closeness made her hands tremble.

'*Ouch!*'

'Damn it, what are you thinking about?' He grasped her wrist. 'Now look what you've done!'

She couldn't look down at her finger with the blood swiftly welling.

'We'll have to put. . . .' He broke off suddenly, looking at her face. 'You faint on me and I'll give you a good beating!'

'You're such a big man too,' she said dryly.

Without fuss he pulled her to her feet, hauling her after him as they made directly through the radio room to the first-aid room beyond. Laura didn't even make a fuss when he lifted her by the waist and propped her up on the white-sheeted couch.

'When I was a little girl I used to flake out at all the grisly bits.'

'I gathered that.' He gave her a sharp look, but her colour had returned. 'If you'll just manage to keep your head up and look over my shoulder, I'll clean this up.'

'Mrs Hunter will wonder what's happened.'

'And she's not used to being abandoned. There, that's about it! You'll be able to report back to Jamie that you survived a gruelling ordeal.'

'Jamie,' she said shakily, and gave a violent sigh. 'I haven't asked you what's happening.'

Blaise studied her in silence for a moment. 'No, you're a strange girl.'

'I know.' With a little laugh she looked away from him, afraid to keep her head tilted to his. It seemed irrational to be madly in love with him when he annoyed her so violently.

'Would you like Jamie to come here?' he asked.

The surprise was so devastating she spun her head back so the silky mass of it belled out. 'I can't believe what you're saying. How would Paula let him?'

'It's what we suspected, Laura. We have your step-mother over a barrel. I think I can promise you with certainty that you'll be allowed to see your brother quite often.'

Her silvery eyes seemed to be swallowing her face. 'You mean he could come *here* for a holiday?'

'Why not?' Unexpectedly he brushed a lock of hair from her face, but even then his hand didn't drop, his long fingers wrapping around her nape.

The whole thing seemed to be taking on the elements of a fantasy, the caress of his fingers, the faint, disturbing tenderness in that hard male face.

'You'd do this for me?' she asked with soft poignancy.

'In a way I do quite like you,' he admitted dryly.

'Though you're quite happy to misjudge me.'

'Careful now, Miss Mallory, remember you're only the governess.'

'That's what I came for—to be useful.'

Unaccountably his hand had remained at the nape of her neck, stirring unutterable excitements and an inner tension that held her in uncanny stillness. It was like being completely in his grasp, unable to move. 'I suppose I should go,' she said breathlessly, almost menaced by his turbulent vitality.

'There's nothing stopping you. Nothing at all.' He seemed perfectly relaxed, yet the moment she went to move his hand skeined through her silver-gilt hair.

'Oh, Blaise'—she turned her cheek against his arm.

'So here we are again,' he said grimly, as though it were impossible to deny it.

'I can't fathom you at all.' Now she was leaning her forehead against him, almost blindly nudging his arm with her face.

'Stop it, Laura,' he said curtly.

'I'm sorry.' She came to herself with sudden shame. 'When I wanted to move, you wouldn't let me.' Her voice was almost a sob and incredibly he couldn't handle it.

He shook her so that her hair flew across her face, his black eyes blazing, so she knew he was at the extreme edge of his limit, but just as she only wanted to collapse against him he jerked up her head and brought down his mouth.

From violence, a lightning transition to a heart-stopping hunger, surrender sweeping over her so she lifted her arms to fling them around his neck. Her need for him was deep and wrenching, unsatisfied, to be eaten away with desire . . . on fire.

His mouth at last freed her and she arched her throat back as his head dipped to the silky crevice behind her ear, his lips trailing down her neck so slowly she wanted to cry out, the torture was as much as she could take. Her whole body was beating the rapid rhythm of her pulse.

'*Blaise.*'

His hands enveloped her small breasts, the thumbs tracing the outline of the aroused nipples, and she shivered violently, her parted mouth taking in a lungful of the exquisite male scent of him. 'I have to go away from you,' she cried.

'Do you want to?' He looked directly into her eyes.

'I w-want . . . I want. . . .'

'To be with me naked. Don't be ashamed to say it.'

'But I *am* ashamed.' She put her hands over his, but still he didn't remove them from her breasts. 'I've never felt like this before. I don't even know if I *want* to feel like this. To be so dominated I'll do anything you want.'

'Would you marry me?'

'Dear lord!' she said beneath her breath. How could he make such a proposal looking like that, hard and purposeful as though he was clinching an important business deal?

'Would you, Laura?' he asked ironically, 'with *my* past?'

'I can't take this in,' she said dazedly.

'Forgive me, my dear, but you can. This isn't the time to be putting on any act. Some things are final.'

'But we're strangers!' She went on protesting, though the time for protesting was past.

'No, Laura, that won't do.' He laughed briefly. 'There might be a lot of things we don't know about each other, but strangers we're not. Think about it for a moment, and don't run away from it. No one can do that for long. Including me. I knew with certainty you would affect my life that first day at Howard's office. You weren't indifferent either, though you didn't want to look at me.'

'But that was *conquest*,' she said vaguely.

'Oh, really?'

'I want a man who loves me.'

'I don't know what one could say for love,' he said sombrely. 'Your body's mine—now and for ever, if I say so.'

'I shouldn't let this astonish me.' She was watching him with an intense, almost fearful concentration. 'You're too much man for me. I have to call a halt.'

'My poor foolish little virgin!' Blaise lifted her from the couch and set her on her feet. 'Fight it for a day or so, then let me know. A few people might find it shocking, but my grandmother won't be one of them. And it seems to me she's waited quite long enough for her brandy.'

'But I couldn't mean less to you,' she protested.

'I mean really. . . .'

He watched her floundering with detached curiosity. 'You need me, Laura, and I need you. We'll discuss the rest of it at another time.'

'I'm not a project,' she told him urgently at the door.

'Not at all.' His black eyes slipped over her. 'You're a necessity. I won't let it hurt too much.'

CHAPTER EIGHT

LAURA awakened the next morning thinking the preceding night had been a dream. Had Blaise really asked her to marry him? The shock of it, the terrible joy of it, was stunning. He didn't love her; she couldn't accept that he loved her. Not as she loved him. That was a woman thing; a love without qualifications and conditions. Could he possibly share the same rapture as she felt in his arms? If he didn't, he was a master of deception, but physical desire was a thing apart . . . his mouth against her own, her body lying still in his arms. She turned over violently as though to be free of the memory, then she twisted back, feeling the same flame. To have him possess her completely would be an agony of pleasure. A pulse began to beat in her throat.

When she went in to breakfast, both Judith and Steven were there, looking up to greet her very pleasantly.

'Well, Laura,' Steven said meaningfully, 'our guests have gone. Now perhaps Blaise will let you out.'

'Oh, thank goodness for that!' Laura felt an instant

wave of relief. 'Did you know Liza had to go for help yesterday?'

'Such a peasant!' Judith said contemptuously. 'I don't think he's come up against anyone like Blaise in his life.'

'I hope it didn't affect the buying trip?' Laura walked to the long sideboard and poured herself some apple juice.

'Oh, hell, it was like this,' Steven laughed. 'They can keep their offers as long as Landers is a member of the syndicate.'

'Good grief!' Laura sat down, dismayed.

'Don't worry, Laura,' Judith said kindly. 'We're not exactly short of buyers, you know.'

'But I somehow feel it was *my* fault.'

Steven leaned across the table and gave an expressive grin. 'Obviously my brother wasn't having you bothered. He kinda made that very plain! Besides, Landers doesn't run the syndicate and the rest of them have a lot of respect for Blaise. No one can act the feudal baron better than he can—born to rule, to tolerate his less patrician fellow men. He kept Landers pretty silent, at any rate.'

'I'm glad he's gone,' Laura murmured quietly.

'So has Blaise.' Judith seemed anxious to offer this piece of information. 'He flew out . . . just exactly . . .' she turned her wrist and glanced at her Piaget watch, 'ten minutes ago.'

'I had no idea.'

'Where he was going we couldn't find out. Nobody knows,' Steven uttered solemnly. 'I just hope nothing comes up.'

'Haven't you the experience to handle it?' Judith demanded shortly.

'My dear,' Steven's brown eyes were bland, 'the men

brush my orders off. Just think, if there wasn't Blaise, there would soon be no station. Guys like Landers would be swarming in to buy it.'

'Oh, stop that, Steven, it's not funny!'

'Darling, it's what you can expect. My brother and I aren't even of the same race of men.'

'Oh, well,' Judith said languidly, 'do the best you can. At least he said we could have a fortnight in Sydney as soon as he gets back. I think I might run amok. Possibly have an affair!'

'You'd better not!' Steven slapped his table napkin down very vigorously. 'You've got one loving guy of your own.'

Judith stared up at him in silence for a moment, then blushed. 'You mean that?'

'Come to think of it, why don't we have a second honeymoon?' He bent over her, grasped her springy curls and kissed her mouth. 'Two weeks is plenty of time.'

'To do what, for instance?'

'To suit ourselves. Let's say instead of Sydney, we try the Great Barrier Reef? You love the water.'

Clearly Judith was intrigued, and she looked up at her husband wonderingly. 'It's an idea, darling. Let's see what Blaise has to say.'

'Book in any case,' Steve said wryly. 'It will give you something to do.'

As it turned out, immediately Blaise turned his back, the station had a run of mishaps. Tomahawk, the part-aboriginal horsebreaker, took a punishing kick from a brumby that put him out of action, Smiler, the old drover, had an unfortunate encounter with a wild camel and complained of double vision, two inexperienced stock boys allowed a bunch of valuable fats to get away from them into the hill country where they could hide away for weeks, and Mrs Madden, cradling

a tray for old Mrs Hunter, fell down the stairs she had
safely negotiated for more than twenty years and afterwards had to drag herself out on to the verandah to cry
for help.

'A mistake, as it happened,' she told Laura later.
The two houseboys who had run to her assistance bore
her from the floor manfully but soon succumbed to
the tremendous strain, one of them falling backwards
into the garden, where he lay unable to get up.

'We'd better send for the doctor,' Judith said with a
sinking heart. 'So many victims, it's ridiculous!'

'I can't go to hospital. *Preposterous!*' Mrs Madden
wailed.

'We'll have a full plane!' Doctor Meade from Base
Hospital cut short her remonstrances. 'I don't like old
Smiler's double vision. I think he's going blind.'

'What on earth are we going to do?' Judith asked
helplessly after the doctor had flown out. 'I really don't
know much about cooking. We always had Grace at
home.'

'But surely we only have to fend for ourselves?'
Laura was trying to distract herself from the memory
of Mrs Madden's rebellious face. 'Dusty cooks for the
men, thank goodness.'

'Well, Steven likes a good breakfast and a good
dinner,' Judith announced in a firm, wifely tone. 'I
mean, he's used to it.'

'We'll manage.' Laura looked at the older girl nonplussed. What was the big deal about getting a few
meals? It made her realise how having a housekeeper
changed things. At least Jean had always been good
showing her how to do things, just as Liza and Mrs
Madden had many heart-to-heart discussions on vari-
ous cookbooks. 'I can always get up and cook breakfast.'

'Oh, would you?' Judith looked immensely relieved. 'Lunch won't be any problem and I'll help you with dinner as best I can.'

'Oh, poor old Annie!' Mrs Hunter was most shaken about their housekeeper's accident. 'She'll hate hospital, you know. She won't give them a minute's peace.'

'Well, you heard what the doctor said,' Laura answered, somewhat upset herself. 'He would have to take an X-ray. I didn't realise an ankle *could* swell up to that size.'

'And poor Smiler!' the old lady made sounds of distress. 'The injuries, concussions he's suffered. It would be just dreadful if he went blind, though God knows it's not unheard-of out here.'

'I wonder what Blaise will think of it all,' Laura ventured, not even noticing her slip over his Christian name.

'One does miss him.'

'Yes.'

As a conversation it was highly revealing, though neither woman appeared to notice it. What made it so, Laura later realised, was that they both looked on him as a sort of god.

Liza, though she expressed much concern that Annie had hurt herself, was thrilled to be given the opportunity to help Laura in the kitchen. It was not perhaps what Laura wanted, given Liza's innocent awkwardness, but she simply didn't have the heart to banish the child from the kitchen.

'Plain flour, dear—that's self-raising,' she felt obliged to point out, whereupon Liza in her efforts to please spread herself and the contents of the packet all over the floor.

All in all there was a pile-up of such setbacks and a

staggering amount of spillage, but Laura managed to meet it all with patient good humour. No one in the household complained, at any rate, and Steven went so far as to call her 'excessively domesticated as, say, opposed to my wife'. Judith only smiled wryly, a young woman used to a fleet of servants all her life.

'I could do it, you know, if I tried,' she told him.

'Why don't you, then?' Liza piped up distinctly, and Judith stared at her as though this harmless little child could one day sit in judgment.

'That was a little rude, Liza,' Laura told her later. 'I mean, you ought not to criticise your Aunt Judith.'

Liza's sandy eyebrows rose in amazement. 'Yeah, well, she might start helping us for a start. We have our work cut out trying to cope.'

At that, Laura gave up. Judith had promised to lend a helping hand, instead of which she invented all manner of excuses to keep her out of the kitchen.

'Claudia's coming back,' she informed them the next morning.

'Oh, no!'

'I'm terribly sorry, yes.' Judith looked at the younger girl in sympathy. 'As far as I'm concerned you can let her fend for herself. Claudia makes no attempt to fit in and she has her head filled with grandiose visions of being mistress of Hunter's Moon.'

'She hasn't got a chance.' Steven looked at his bacon and eggs a bit critically.

'I'm sorry the bacon's too crisp,' Laura apologised.

'Think nothing of it,' Steven put his arm around her shoulders. 'If Claudia is flying in, I'll be out for the rest of the day.'

'*Steven!*'

'I might as well,' he grizzled, 'seeing your sister and

I don't hit it off. Did you know she once called me a misfit?'

'She should keep her mouth shut,' Judith said violently, 'but of course she won't. I must say it's Blaise who's keeping her slightly deranged. Why doesn't he marry someone and put her out of her misery?'

'You know damned well my brother baulks the Big One.' Suddenly Steven sounded glum. 'One unhappy marriage is pretty destructive. I suppose the next time he'll pick some innocent little creature who can be relied on to do her duty and not press for attention. Even if he doesn't love her, it won't matter. She'll just accept what she gets as a magnificent gift.'

'You know,' Judith pointed out wonderingly, 'you're jealous of Blaise.'

'Not jealous,' Steven said slowly, his brown eyes shadowed. 'Envious, perhaps. A little resentful. Blaise has always called the tune and I've always followed after. It is as it should be, but it scarcely makes me happier.'

'Then why don't you do what *you* want to do?' Laura challenged him. 'Life doesn't wait on us, we have to seize the moment.'

'Are you suggesting treason?' Steven asked quietly.

'Why not talk to your brother about how you feel? He might be . . . autocratic,' Laura hesitated, searching for a word that might best describe Blaise and not happy with the one she found, but Steven burst out laughing.

'Are you criticising my brother?' he demanded.

'Bear with me, I'm only trying to find a word to describe him.'

'You've come pretty close,' Steven was still chuckling. 'What's it mean anyway, absolute ruler? I daresay he's that.'

'And he's indisputably highly intelligent, and surely it has occurred to you, a most reasonable man.'

'Are we supposed to tell him we don't want to live on Hunter's Moon?' Judith asked.

'Well, do you?'

Judith's face was a study. She glanced at her husband, then back at Laura. 'Would *you*?' she countered briskly.

'But it's a fabulous place!'

'My God, she means it!' Judith told her husband soberly. 'Isn't that stunning.'

'But it *is*.' Laura was amazed anyone could find it otherwise. 'Why, it speaks to me—the pearly dawns and the sunsets, this great limitless ancient land, the legions of birds, the shimmering mirage, the tribal legends and sacred places, the great herds of cattle. Could there be a more beautiful spot than Paradise Pool or a more barbaric splendour than the desert? And I haven't even seen it after the rains!'

'*Then* it's fabulous,' Judith amended, looking into Laura's glowing eyes. 'Wildflowers clear away to the horizon, but actually, if you want the truth, I find it overwhelming. The wonders of nature never did interest me a great deal. I'm country bred but a city girl at heart. Claudia is the one who understands this life, and she's mad about horses—something she and Blaise have in common. If I really had a choice I would want to live in Sydney, somewhere on that glorious blue harbour. I look on water the way people look on the bush. But we'd never be allowed to go.'

'Why not?'

'Oh, Laura!' Judith dropped her glossy dark head. 'You don't understand. Nothing is easy in the family, the financial set-up. We're rich while we're here, and Blaise does need Steven, you know. At least he's one hundred per cent devoted to his brother's interests.'

'You could at least speak to Blaise,' Laura persisted. 'I'm sure he hasn't the faintest idea Steven is such a gifted writer.'

'Oh, that!' said Judith in a faintly weary voice. 'Who makes money writing short stories?'

'It seems to me you have all the material—the vivid, first-hand descriptions for a big read.' Laura addressed Steven directly.

'Another *Thorn Birds*?' Judith asked sarcastically.

'Don't you think I could do it?' Steven demanded, little points of anger sparking his eyes. 'Have you read some of my stuff, Laura?'

'Your grandmother lent me your big manuscript, and I enjoyed it immensely. With a little editing I'm sure you could even find a publisher. There's so much that's fascinating about Outback life, and your action sequences are very good. It's all your first-hand knowledge and you can turn it to account.'

'Don't encourage him, Laura.' Judith shook her head. 'It will never work out. The station is a monster that devours all of us.'

'I could sell out to Blaise.' Steven was momentarily on fire, his old ambitions resurrected in the face of Laura's support.

'And where would that leave us?' Judith cried aggressively. 'Rich for a couple of years. With our life-style we need big money constantly coming in. How much do you think the right house on the Harbour would cost? Anything around the two or three million mark, maybe more. Forget the writing, unless you really can turn out a blockbuster. It's not easy, that's for sure.'

'And it's not hard either!' Steven fired. 'Look at that rubbishy thing you were reading.'

'A woman's book,' Judith defended her choice.

'I can do better than that.' Steven stood up huffily, preparing to leave.

'Then *do* it,' Laura told him levelly.

'Oh, please, please don't encourage him,' Judith sighed worriedly after Steven had left. 'I know he has talent, but surely talent isn't enough?'

'How's he going to feel happy with himself, Judith, if he doesn't give it a go? I don't say he could turn out a phenomenon, and yet I'm not sure he couldn't. The thing is, I couldn't stop reading his stories until I'd finished, and I have some critical faculty—at least I've been told so. Hasn't he got a right to fulfilment?'

'Only as long as he can bring in the money,' Judith said shortly. 'I haven't mentioned it to anyone else yet, but I think I'm pregnant,' she went on.

'Why, that's wonderful!'

'I don't know what to think at the moment. I'm going to hate losing my figure.'

'But think of the reward!'

'I suppose it will be wonderful,' Judith said uncertainly. 'One presupposes every woman is cut out to be a mother, but really, I'm not sure. Parenthood isn't as easy as all that. And what if something is wrong with the marriage? Is having a baby going to make it any better?'

'I'm sure Steven will be thrilled,' Laura reassured her quietly.

'I don't know if he will. Steven mightn't fight for himself, but he could put up a fight for his children. I don't know what the station symbolises to him. Impossible standards, I think. He can't live up to it, and his children might find it a burden as well. You can see why we both want Blaise to get married. The chances of his having a son in the same mould are about ninety-five per cent, and it would take the pressure off us. I'm no great shakes as a member of a great pioneering family and neither is Steven. Blaise is the one who should be producing the next heir. He could have just about any woman he wanted. You want to see it when we have some big function on the station. They *fight* for him! I mean, literally they come to blows. And Claudia has told them all to lay off. Poor Claudia! She has no chance with Blaise, you know, but she won't be told. It's like a terrible mental block with her. I think she'd kill the woman who tried to take him off her.'

'How alarming!' said Laura wryly.

'Shocking, but that's the way she is about him.'

'Then he must have given her cause,' Laura said with enormous conviction and a terrible sinking feeling.

'Who knows?' Judith stared off into space. 'Who knows anything with Blaise? We tell him everything and he tells us nothing. We don't even know where he is now. He could be picking out a bride in Adelaide for all we know. There are lots of people he knows, and I don't think he's exactly what you'd call a saint. Why, he even used to get me excited in the old days, but I had to turn it off as soon as Steven noticed. A harmless thing, really. Just a fantasy. Blaise has never noticed me, and I think the shock of Virginia's death has been remorseless. She was the most stunning woman – an extraordinary creature. She was a kind of one-off and I suppose we must be grateful for that. I suppose whatever she did, Blaise has never forgotten her.'

'Liza never speaks about her mother,' Laura said with deep sadness.

'Virginia had no time for the child. In actual fact, she was quite cruel. Liza, funny little thing that she is, apparently made her own decision not to suffer. She's really quite stoic. She realised her mother was different, so she gave all her devotion to Blaise. And he's been absolutely magnificent to that child. I could never do it. I would have had to send her away to her grandparents.'

'But they didn't want her either.'

'Which just goes to show you blood isn't as thick as the milk of human kindness.'

There was an awkward silence and Judith got up. 'If there's nothing I can do for you, Laura, I'll go and see to Claudia's room. I wish I could find a way of telling her there's nothing to be gained by all these visits and she's ignoring the fact that a girl should have her pride. Or more accurately, Blaise will pick his own woman in his own time. He has a will of iron and the power to back it up.'

Laura tidied away with a head full of anxieties and a heavy heart. Into her mind swam Steven's words . . . *an innocent little creature who can be relied on to do her duty*. . . . What exactly was that duty? To provide an heir? Obviously one was needed or a historic station would one day fall into the hands of a syndicate. Was it a case of surrendering one's body for the purposes of procreation in exchange for a wedding ring and a privileged, lonely life?

No chance of *that*! she whispered to herself. She wasn't going to accept a few crumbs and be grateful for them. She wanted a marriage, the most perfect alliance. She thought she was well balanced enough to accept the demands running a big station would have on Blaise, but she could never accept that he wouldn't long to come home to her in the evenings.

'He can think again!' she said aloud.

'Gosh, Laura, are you talking to yourself?' Liza, loitering until her Aunt Judith had finished, raced around the door.

'I am addressing the wall,' Laura answered, determined not to be flustered.

'And what did it say?'

'It said it looks like we're going to have another visitor. Claudia.'

Liza tried but failed to shut up. 'What more ills are to befall us?'

'I wonder if you could hold that door open for me, sweetie?' she sighed.

'I hope she doesn't think we're going to cook for her,' Liza said.

Claudia, an experienced pilot, flew in in her father's Cessna and two hours later, to everyone's unbounded relief, the Beech Baron touched down on the all-weather runway.

'It's Blaise. It's *Blaise*!' Liza waved frantically at the brilliant, cloudless sky. 'Oh, enter your domain, Lord of the Western Skies!'

Laura, looking at her, was much amused. 'I think we might try a quick trot back to the stables.'

'Let's gallop, don't you mean!' Liza, starry-eyed, kneed her pony. 'I wonder what he's brought me back? Last time it was that computer game. He just knew I'd get the hang of it.'

Though the ride back to the stables complex was as exhilarating as any they had tried together, Blaise had obviously beaten them back, for the yellow jeep stood at the base of the stairs and one of the houseboys was carrying up two cases of luggage.

'You don't think he's brought someone with him, do you suppose?' Liza was eyeing the unfamiliar, inexpensive luggage.

'I don't know, I'm sure.' Laura was beginning to feel strange, a sense of portent that had her hurrying up the short flight of marble stairs.

'What about *me*?' Liza called after her in a jolly manner, and just as Laura reached the portico, a small boy ran out of the entrance hall and straight into Laura's outstretched arms.

'*Jamie!*' she shrieked.

'Laura. *Laura!*' He was there, gold hair, flushed cheeks, a little thinner and taller, her own darling brother.

'Oh, Jamie!' Laura gathered the beloved body into her arms. 'If this isn't the most wonderful surprise!'

'It's true!' he exclaimed. 'Mr Hunter brought us in his own plane, and there's Jean.'

Laura lifted her head and Jean's dear familiar plump figure appeared on the scene.

'Lovey.'

Now all three of them were huddled together, hugging and smiling, the two women dashing back the happy tears.

'It seems like a miracle!' Laura exclaimed.

'A miracle called Hunter,' Jean said in her ear.

Liza was hovering and Laura turned back smilingly and put out her hand. 'Liza dear, surely you know who this is?'

'It's Jamie.' Like a flash Liza put out her hand. 'Hi, Jamie, I've heard all about you.'

'Who spilled ink on you, Liza?'

'Oh, I did that myself this morning.'

'And this is Miss Frazer, Liza. A very dear friend of mine.'

'Och, *Jean!*' the woman protested.

'Then I'm happy to know you, Jean.'

'It's a mighty fine girl you are with those roses in your cheeks.'

'We've just been galloping,' Liza informed her.

'Shall I tell you about Honey, Jamie?' She turned on the younger child radiantly.

'Next year I'm going to riding school,' Jamie announced. 'How old are you, Liza?'

'Eight.' Liza was looking at him with a warm friendship. 'Have you come for a holiday?'

'A whole month!' Jamie suddenly grabbed Laura's hand and kissed it, the expression on his face so happy and excited Laura wanted to cry.

'Then we're going to make it the best holiday of all time.' Liza placed a small brown hand on Jamie's golden head. 'We'll go swimming and riding and exploring and Blaise might let us camp out a few nights. I'll keep an eye on you, don't worry.'

'Are there kangaroos?'

'Tons of them,' Liza seized his arm. 'Do you know how a big a joey is when it's born?'

Blaise was inside the entrance hall, looking straight at her, and the sight of him was so intimate she wanted to rush to him and fling herself into his arms. Instead she stood still and thanked him with her heart in her glowing eyes.

'I knew you'd be pleased.' He smiled at the children, who had come to stand close to him, Liza leaning her head against his side.

'Pleased isn't an adequate word.' She hadn't quite got control over her voice. 'I'm just so grateful.'

'And Jean here wants a cup of tea,' he said lightly, giving her the moment to blink back the tears. 'Come to that, I'd like coffee and I'm sure the children would like a cold drink.'

'This is a very important house, isn't it, Mr Hunter?' Jamie said solemnly.

'The welcoming kind.' He glanced down at the small boy with some kind of reflectiveness in him so that

Laura became aware for the first time that he really did want a son.

'If you like, Jamie,' Liza said, 'I'll show you around it now.'

'Oh, great! I love houses. When I grow up I'm going to be an architect. My father was an engineer, did you know? But I'd sooner build houses than bridges.'

'What about a drink first?' Laura asked.

'I've heard about Mrs Madden's accident,' Jean said with the voice of efficiency. 'I want to help out in every way I can. I won't be happy playing the lady.'

'I still want you to relax and enjoy yourself, Jean,' Blaise Hunter said firmly.

'And that's what I'll do. Perhaps, Laura, you can show me the kitchen. I'll vacate it the very moment your Mrs Madden returns.'

'I shall come down for dinner,' old Mrs Hunter announced when Laura took the children to visit her suite. As she spoke she moved her hand and Jamie leaned forward to make the fascinated observation,

'Gosh, Mrs Hunter, that diamond must weigh a ton!'

'My engagement ring, Jamie.' She twisted her hand so the great diamond flashed again and again.

'It must have cost a lot of money.'

'Yes,' she said calmly. 'I feel so much better tonight. Why don't we have an early dinner, then the children can eat with us as a special treat?'

'Hey, we can get all the silver out!' Liza said excitedly.

'No, you won't!' Laura shook her head. 'We're not using anything I can't put through the dishwasher!'

Mrs Hunter glanced at her and laughed. 'I know you've been bearing the load, and very competent you are too.'

'Well, I've had Liza to help me,' Laura said smilingly, 'and Marilyn and Kate when I can get them to pull themselves together.'

'It's very good of you, Laura,' Mrs Hunter said gratefully. 'And I'll remember. Now, help me choose something to wear for dinner. I'm looking forward to meeting your nice Jean.'

Dinner turned out to be a very happy and festive occasion. Jean turned out a simple but elegant meal, a sort of compromise between adults and children, and afterwards sat down with them, while Blaise was simply charming to her. His mood light and teasing, Steven plied Jamie with questions and he answered very neatly, much to Laura's pleasure.

Tonight happiness had made her incandescent, so that looking across the table Claudia experienced a surge of pure hatred. Of course the girl was trouble, she had known that from the beginning. Now she must decide what to do. No governess could sit there and look so overwhelmingly eye-catching. She was even wearing pearls with her glowing amber dress, and Claudia, staring, knew those pearls were real. How dared she! Who *was* she? Claudia glanced away to find old Mrs Hunter staring straight at her, her gaze level and not shifting for long minutes.

After that, Claudia took the trouble to be nice to the children who, from the expressions on their faces, found it amazing. They studied Claudia's haughty, beautifully tanned face doubtfully and turned away in relief as soon as someone else asked a question or passed some remark.

Afterwards they walked arm in arm up the stairway with Liza, a great talker, discussing what books they might look at before it was time for bed. Jamie, instead of being intimidated by a huge room of his own,

seemed thrilled, and when Laura suggested he might
like a nightlight he bounced up and down on the impressive fourposter and laughed.

'I don't want anything at all, Laura. See the moonlight!'

Liza hurried in with her nightdress on. 'We can leave
all the connecting doors open, in any case.'

'I love this place,' Jamie said sweetly, and tugged
his sister down on the bed. 'I've missed you, Laura. I
wanted to come to you all the time.'

'*Darling!*' She gathered him up, grateful he was not
yet at the age when a sister's kisses had to be rubbed
off. 'I missed you too, but we're going to see one another lots of times.'

'Mummy said she'd love to come out here some
time.' Jamie settled into Laura's lap and Liza hopped
up on the bed companionably.

'Did she really?' Laura couldn't have been more
amazed.

'Can she?' Jamie asked. 'She's never really happy
without me.'

'It's Mr Hunter's house, Jamie.'

'Oh, Blaise would be agreeable,' Liza said vigorously. 'He'd do anything for Laura.'

'I don't know about that, dear,' Laura stammered.

'Oh, he *would*, Laura,' Liza informed her sedately.
'Any time you ask him Jamie's mother can come
out.'

'And he's the pilot of his own plane!' Jamie cried, as
though he could think of absolutely nothing more
remarkable.

'Can I stay here with Jamie until he goes to sleep?'
Liza asked. 'I love talking in the dark.'

'Then we'll turn off the light now.'

Within moments, while Liza waxed lyrical about

what they were going to do the next day Jamie, an
over-excited four-year-old, tumbled into Dreamworld.

'Isn't he a sweet little kid?' Liza sighed. 'When I
grow up I'm going to have six—no, wait, ten children.'

'At least have two,' Laura said, and taking her by
the hand escorted Liza back to her own room where
she curled up in bed and lay back on the pillows.

'I should say this was a lovely day, wouldn't you?'
smiled Liza.

'Lovely.' Laura bent down and kissed her with real
affection.

'Why not stay here all the time?' Liza suggested.
'Blaise certainly won't mind.'

Laura had nothing to say to that. 'Goodnight, dear,'
she said lightly. 'God bless.'

'God bless you too, Laura.' Liza became very serious
and fervent. 'Better get some sleep, because us kids are
going to be up early in the morning.'

She met Steven on the stairs and he looked at her
quizzically. 'What are you smiling about?'

'Liza,' she regarded him with sparkling eyes. 'She's
the most engaging child.'

'I guess she has her moments,' Steven nodded his
head. 'Listen,' he reached out and suddenly grasped
her wrist, 'did you mean what you said about my writing?'

'I did, Steven. You're good. But if you want a highly
qualified opinion I can get you one. I know James
Garrison quite well.'

'You know James Garrison?' Steven's brown eyes
warmed into excitement and his whole expression
altered. 'How do *you* know such a famous writer?'

'I lived next door to his sister nearly all my life.
She's a lovely person. I was in and out of her house all

the time, and of course we always saw James whenever he came home to Australia. He's the most interesting, brilliant man, and just as nice as he could be. I know he'd be kind enough to look at your work and give an opinion. He's like that. He's not all wrapped up in himself. He helps people.'

'Could he help *me*?' Carried away, Steven scooped her up in his arms and stared down at her incredulously.

'He'd certainly tell you whether it was worth it or not to take the gamble.'

'You angel!' He bent his dark head and kissed her cheek resoundingly. 'If you pull this off I'll love you for ever and ever.'

'Amen,' a dark, resonant voice said suavely. 'Are you coming downstairs again, Miss Mallory?'

'Down you go!' Steven told her happily. 'As far as I'm concerned it's bed. We have to be up at four in the morning.'

'I'm sure the children will wake you,' Laura said.

Blaise was waiting for her at the bottom of the stairs. 'Do you mean to tell me what that was all about?'

'No,' she shook her head lightly. 'Steven can tell you.'

'As long as you don't plan on running off together.'

'You say that as if you'd murder me,' Laura commented.

'It's very good to know where one stands.' He spoke the words so carelessly, yet she felt her heart jump. The tone didn't match the deliberation in his formidable face.

'Hey, it was just a friendly discussion,' she said swiftly.

'I'd rest a lot easier if you weren't quite so lovable.'

'I'd better go and help Jean,' she said carefully.

'Jean doesn't want any help. She just told me.' He took her arm and all but propelled her through the open double doorway. 'Come for a walk, if you don't mind.'

She looked up at him, startled. 'But what about the others?'

'Others?' Blaise looked down his arrogant nose at her. 'My grandmother has retired for the night. Claudia and Judith are busy biting one another's heads off and you've already kissed Steven good-night.'

'You don't have to keep such a grip on me,' she said, feigning a little moan.

'I'm sorry. But it's to your advantage to come quietly.'

The night was superb, a fantastic copper moon that lit up the parkland surrounding the house and turned the stands of trees into mysterious thickets, places of thrall that made her swallow as she approached them. Why were yearnings so much more powerful at night? The first longing seized her, though she moved quietly and gracefully by his side. How terrible if he should catch the scent of desire she thought must come from her skin. For all she knew he would make a consummate lover, he wanted little from women. Little from her except her youth and the innocence that clung to her and made her acceptable.

That he should take her for a fool, though she loved him!

Somewhere, perhaps a few miles from the compound, the Aboriginals were having one of their song festivals. The sound of the tap sticks carried strongly on the fresh air, voices intensifying and dying with the rhythm of the chant. Laura loved the sound of these plaintive love chants, the muffled thrum of the spirit

drums, but tonight they were strangely nerve-tauten-
ing.

When Blaise spoke to her, she jumped.

'What nonsense is this?' He turned her towards him
impatiently.

'I was listening to the chanting. Sometimes they
really sing the night away.'

'Do you want to see it?' he asked.

'I wouldn't want to intrude on them.'

That made him laugh. 'My people love an audi-
ence,' he said quietly. 'It isn't far. We'll take the
jeep.'

'But what about. . . .'

'Do you want me to slap you?'

She wanted him to do far more than that. 'You're
giving me the impression you'd find it easy.'

'*Please*, Laura,' he said in a profoundly disturbing
voice.

'Then lead on.'

The song group welcomed them warmly, their glossy
black faces alive with pure joy. An upright old man
with grey curls above his high forehead came forward
and extended the greeting on behalf of his people and
Blaise responded gravely, extending his arm and placing it on the old man's shoulder.

Laura stood behind him demurely, much, she
realised, in the order of this ancient tribe, and a small
child with an eager beaming face suddenly broke away
from the circle of his mother's arms and rushed up to
her to tell her his name.

'Mitja,' he indicated himself with a thumb gestured
towards his chest.

'Laura.'

His girlish mother was after him in a flash, but not
before Laura had shaken the small, extended hand.

'Mitja,' the mother smiled at Laura shyly, but delivered a spanking slap to Mitja's small rear.

'*Hush!*' The old fellow, who was clearly a tribal elder, frowned on them both and they melted back to the seated circle around the fire that had been lit.

Someone had found a skin for them to sit down on and for a half hour or more they sat listening to the tribal lullabies that had flowed into the Inland air since long before the white man arrived with his sheep and cattle. Such songs were precious, part of an ancient heritage, and nothing gave them more pleasure than to congregate and sing of the days when the tribes were once mighty.

'I enjoyed that,' Laura said later, her voice lilting. 'I think I might get them to sing to me every day, like all the old chieftains had bards. It's good to sing of heroes and gods and brave deeds and, of course, love chants. Everyone wants to hear a love song.'

'Even when they're doleful?'

'Ah, well, there are plenty of them around.'

The night breeze was wreathed with a myriad scents and as they walked back to the jeep, rustlings in the grass.

'Don't panic,' said Blaise as she all but fell against him.

'I should tell you I have a horror of snakes,' said Laura.

'As they have of people. You'd have to be fairly unlucky to tread on real trouble, though even a small snake can deliver a nasty drop of venom. Certainly enough to make you sick for a few days.'

'Oh, thank you.' She didn't care what he thought, she took his arm.

'Shall I carry you?' he offered.

'I can walk.'

'Careful now where you put your feet.'

'Damn it, you're doing this on purpose!'

'Yes.' His voice was deep and amused.

'How *could* you!'

'Easily. Maybe I like you clinging to me.'

'Not *you*, Blaise,' Laura said ruefully.

'So you keep saying.'

'All right,' she said wryly, 'but not for always. Just when *you* feel like it.'

'Feel like what?'

He turned to her and in the bright moonlight she could see his eyes glittering.

'Oh, I don't know.' She felt totally defeated by this extraordinary man, who alternated between kissing her breathless and keeping her firmly in her place. 'Please allow me to thank you for all you've done for me,' she said passionately. 'Jean told me about your meetings with my stepmother. You're a very clever man to achieve the impossible.'

'When she was looking down a gunbarrel!' He gave a brief, explosive laugh. 'Quite frankly, Laura, I'd like to see her punished as she deserves, but then we'd lose much more than we gained. Jamie needs his mother. She does love him, at least, and we must avoid a scandal. The story will never be told, though no doubt a lot of people have their suspicions. Justice has been done, and you may be sure I'll keep an eye on Paula until her dying day. You're going to have your cake, golden girl, and eat it too. We may even allow your dear stepmother to have a week or so with her rich relations. She'd love that, and if it keeps things rosy for you and Jamie I don't mind. She's a strange woman anyway.'

'I'm sure of that,' Laura jerked out. 'I suppose she treated you like her dearest friend.'

'Quite unbelievable. You'd think she'd been caught out in a trifling misdemeanour. Women actually confound me completely.'

'As for men, they never do a thing wrong.'

'They can generally be relied upon to act in a more honourable fashion.'

Laura moaned. 'Well, thank you anyway.'

'You can.'

The way he said it made her draw a shaky breath. She tried to get in the jeep, but Blaise held her prisoner.

'Thank me now.' His voice was amused with the faintest brush of violence.

'I thought I had.'

'Not good enough.' He turned her so she faced into his arms. 'I'm not going to let you go until I get full value.'

'You can't mean that,' she whispered. 'Not with Claudia waiting for you back at the house.'

'Claudia hasn't got what you've got.'

'And you're in a position to make the comparison?' Despite herself a faint bitterness crept into her voice.

'Do you mean,' he asked in a perfectly hard and steady tone, 'have I made love to Claudia?'

'It's entirely your own business.'

'I'd rather it didn't come between us,' he said loftily. 'Claudia as far as I'm concerned is an in-law, and I do not conduct affairs with the in-laws.'

'But you *do* conduct them?'

'In some style at least,' he said with silky distinctness. 'Didn't you know, Laura, that I'm a very eligible man?'

'So why pick on an obscure governess?'

'But you're not, are you? You're a well bred young lady who can now afford to leave me if she wants to.'

'Why should you want me?' she asked seriously. 'I

have absolutely no intention of being just a sleeping
partner.'

'*Just* a sleeping partner! My dear girl, I don't re-
commend marriage unless that part of it is going to be
very good.'

'And what about the rest of the time?' She threw her
ash-blonde head up.

'We can do everything together except that you'll
never be allowed to leave home.'

Under the sardonic humour, bitter memories were
breaking through.

'I'm sorry, Blaise,' she said, gently brokenhearted,
'but I could never marry a man who doesn't love me.'

'If I said I loved you, would you be appeased? I
mean, I could say it easily.'

'I don't think you can.' She looked apprehensively
into his jet-black eyes.

'Would you believe I'm hungry for you?'

'Yes.' That part she could feel in the white-hot tension that held them poised.

'Then you begin to see. Kiss me, Laura,' he said
curtly.

It did no good to deny him. She lifted herself up
like a dancer and eased her body into the shape of his.
She wanted to say I love you, love you ... *love you*,
but they weren't words he was ready to hear. She
thought she had it in her to keep her pride high, then
she realised it was all too late. Who else could make
her feel wild, could dominate her so that the prospect
of life with him became frighteningly beautiful?

She touched his mouth with her own, their breaths
mingling, perilously close to whispering of the spell he
had cast on her. His mouth was the most passionate
curve, fervid, though he kept himself under tight control.

'Not here,' he said tersely as though the songsters could suddenly sweep up the bank.

'Where?'

'You in my bed.'

'Impossible!'

'I know. But there are plenty of wide open spaces between here and there.'

Somehow they were in the jeep again, and presently they came to a place like an open circle swathed by heavily foliaged trees like cloaks. 'I'm frightened, Blaise,' Laura said, and her voice shook with excitement.

'So you should be. It's not easy to give yourself over to another human being.'

His magnetism pulled her onwards though there were tremors running right through her body.

'Blaise,' she said in a voice, almost whispering, 'won't everyone wonder where we are?'

'Do you care?' He almost laughed.

'I'd care if they were worried.' He had drawn her into his arms and his hands slid up her smooth back.

'They *will* be worried, Laura,' he told her. 'As worried as hell. I've no doubt Claudia is crying aloud her previous bad opinion of you.'

'Oh, yes,' she said with a flash of temper, 'give *me* the blame!'

'Aren't you to be blamed for weaving so many spells?' He bent his head and pressed his mouth into the hollow of her throat. 'A nice girl like you. The cool and very elegant young lady who looked at me so despairingly at Howard's.'

'I think I cared about you then,' she said wonderingly, feeling the warmth of his mouth moving beneath her chin and the side of her face. 'I thought you were . . . astonishing! So much in command of yourself and

. . . me!' Her voice almost dropped away at the last word.

'Are you going to marry me?' he demanded, and her heart leapt in her breast at the way his arms tightened on her so possessively.

'I don't know,' she said raggedly. 'I can't deny I'm in love with you.'

'Oh, you're right, all right.' Strange leaping lights danced in his eyes. 'You're so weak now I could crush you.'

'What do you want me to marry you for?' she entreated.

'Because without you I'd feel cheated of my only hope in life.'

He wasn't smiling or tender. He was as she had seen him on that first day, a man so formidable he had disturbed her deeply.

'But how can that be possible?' Her widened silvery eyes fastened on him with intensity. 'You have everything!'

'I want you,' he said briefly.

And then he kissed her mouth, though the question remained.

Everything in her flew to him. Her soul. Her spirit. It was as it had been those other times. She couldn't get enough of him. Inhibitions fell away though the force of her own passion confounded her.

'You're extraordinary,' he murmured as they slid together to the soft, scented springy grass. 'Extraordinarily beautiful!'

'My dress!' she gave a little cry.

'Take it off.'

She stared up at him, but his dark face was entirely in shadow. 'This is dangerous, Blaise.'

'I want you deeply.' With deliberate, exquisite care

he helped her remove her dress, then abruptly as she was half turned from him drew her slender, creamy body fully into his arms. 'That's a very pretty slip.'

'I know.'

'I guess it won't come off.'

'I——' She lifted her slim hand to him, vulnerable with the accumulation of many things.

'Your heart is pounding beneath my hand.' He slid his hand over her naked breast.

'I've never done this before,' she said shakily.

'You'd better not.' He bent his head and kissed her to an aching hunger. 'You belong to me. You belong *here*.' He let his hands travel very slowly over her and her body tautened and drew in as his fingers moved over her.

'Oh, Blaise!' She was dimly aware she was crying.

'Don't, darling, I won't force you.'

She had never suspected his voice could hold such deep feeling, and it was her undoing. 'You would never have to force me,' she said and buried her face against his neck. 'I love you. I don't care. I *have* to say it.'

'And I'm supposed to let you go?' His arms closed around her so violently it almost stopped her breath.

Her slip slithered to her waist and though he kissed her repeatedly and fondled her yearning body until she was almost screaming for release he stopped short of possession.

'Tell me you're going to marry me.' He held her heated face firmly.

'Yes, Blaise, you awful man.'

'Tell me you love me again.'

'I love you.'

Tenderness wasn't what he wanted now, and if he didn't *stop*. . . .

He put her away from him though she was still clutching

at him wildly. 'Are you sure you want to stay a virgin until we're married?'

Sanity came back to her for a moment, her long-held beliefs. 'Oh *yes*,' she breathed deeply. 'I suspect you really want that too.'

'Then, Miss Mallory,' he said with a crisp authority, 'I'd better take you back to the house where you'll be safe.'

CHAPTER NINE

IT wasn't until Laura was preparing for bed that she realised with a stab of panic that she didn't have her mother's pearls. Of course Blaise had taken them from her when they kept getting in his way. But did he still have them? She couldn't even remember what he had done with them, such had been the fantastic excitement. But she remembered them now. It would be impossible for her to sleep unless she was certain he had them safe. Apart from their monetary value, which was not inconsiderable, she properly viewed them as something precious, something that had belonged to her mother. Blaise would understand if she went to him and asked him where they were. The children were sleeping deeply; Liza giving the occasional endearing little snore. The household would have settled with Claudia preparing to spend an endless anxiety-racked night.

Poor Claudia! Blaise had made it very clear to her that he had never even contemplated an affair with, as he put it, an in-law, and Blaise being precisely the sort of man he was, Laura believed him. Still, many a man and woman had been known to hope in the face of all logic. Still she felt sorry for Claudia and remembered her face when she and Blaise had walked in. It must have been clear to her that it was the end. Absolutely.

Laura pulled on her soft-as-silk robe, stepped into her bedroom slippers and went to her door, peering out. The lofty, wide gallery was silent and empty with only the soft golden glow of the wall brackets to light it. Blaise had his suite in the other wing. She had never actually seen into it, but she knew where it was.

The door was shut and she tapped gently, well aware he would find it very unusual to find her outside. The cedar doors were so thick and heavy she thought the sound of her tapping would be muffled, so she rapped a little louder.

'Laura.' He came to the door, still dressed, though his ice-blue shirt was open to the waist and his expression, though surprised, didn't indicate that he thought her sudden appearance in her nightclothes was a serious breach of etiquette. 'Changed your mind?'

She opened her eyes wider, the iron hand of excitement clamping on her flesh again. Beyond him she could see a magnificent room, almost opulent in style with its massive, antique furniture. She could see the bed. King-sized.

'So, little one?'

She swallowed and said at last, 'Blaise, have you got my pearls?'

'Hell, what an anti-climax!' he moaned.

'Please, I'm worried.'

'Of course I've got them,' he said gently. 'Are you going to be fool enough to come in and get them?'

'No,' she answered his beautiful smile. 'As long as I know they're safe.'

She turned to go, but he bent his head and kissed

her mouth, tugging her head gently from side to side.
'I want you passionately.'

'I want you too,' she whispered softly.

'Rather awesome, isn't it?'

Whatever she went to answer was lost as a woman's
voice cried out to them, shrivelled in hate.

'Don't keep her standing outside the door, Blaise.
Drag her in!' Claudia stalked towards them and from
the swollen puffiness of her face it was obvious she
had been crying.

'Go to bed, Claudia.' Blaise's voice was so harshly
emphatic it was a wonder it didn't stop her in her tracks.

'You fool, Blaise!' she screeched at him, her full
mouth working. 'Didn't you make one disastrous marriage? Surely you're not contemplating another?'

The handsome face hardened to granite. 'My dear
Claudia,' he said with weary scorn, 'I'm quite willing
to forget this if you'll just go away.'

'I'll bet you haven't told her everything,' Claudia
challenged him.

'I do things *my* way.' The menace wasn't heavy-
handed, but it was surely there.

'Agreed.' She gave a wild laugh.

'Perhaps I should go——' Laura began.

'Stay there.' Claudia flicked her a deadly glance.
'There's a lot you have to know before you mate up
with the Hunters.'

'Maybe I know it, Claudia.' Laura's soft voice held
a tinge of pity.

'I don't think so!' Claudia corrected violently, her
face pale beneath its dark golden tan.

'Is this a private discussion or a free-for-all?'
Steven's sleep-muffled voice suddenly demanded.

'Oh, be quiet, Steven!' Claudia flashed him a backward glance. Judith, pulling on a robe, was behind him,

her face defenceless, then suddenly filled with enormous embarrassment.

'Oh, Claudia,' she went towards her sister. 'What are you doing—saying?'

'Keep out of this!' Claudia exploded.

'She's really off her rocker,' Steven said seriously. His face had lost the dazed look and he glanced from one to the other with instant comprehension. 'So Big Brother has lost his heart at last.'

'We know where his heart is,' Claudia cried wildly. 'It was buried with Virginia. He's never been free since!'

'Look, Claudia,' Judith said violently, 'shut up.'

'Or *be* shut up.' Blaise said pointedly. 'I won't have my grandmother upset or disturbed.'

'And what about this angel-faced little bitch here?' she hurled at him. 'Don't you care about her?'

'I think Laura's more than a match for you.'

'You brute, Blaise!' Claudia suddenly crumpled. 'You've let me love you for years. You've turned me into a mindless zombie only seeing you.'

'I'm sorry, Claudia,' he studied her sombrely, 'but I've never spoken one word to you that could remotely be considered lover-like.'

'You've looked at me,' she said piteously. 'You've smiled at me. You kissed me when I won the big endurance race.'

'I didn't think you'd so distort a casual tribute. You are, after all, family.'

'Oh, Claudia,' Judith said sorrowfully. 'Come to bed—I'll go with you.'

'Forget it.' Claudia appeared to strengthen abruptly. 'There's more business to be discussed tonight.'

'I'll have to hit her, Blaise,' said Steven, his gold-flecked brown eyes serious and wary.

'Does Liza's little governess know. . . .'

'Get one more word out, Claudia,' Blaise snapped grindingly, 'and you'll regret it all your life.'

'*What* life?' she taunted him. 'What life have I got without you?'

'Gosh, this is *sick*!' Steven muttered after a minute. 'You know, Claudia, you'd better get yourself a psychiatrist. Hire him by the week.'

'He would have married me without her!'

'You might as well talk to the wall.' Judith, too, was paper-white, slumping against the panelling.

'Go to bed, love,' Steven told her urgently. 'Go on, *go*. There's nothing to be gained standing here.'

'She's my sister and I've tried to tell her over and over, but she would never listen.'

'And I'm not listening now,' Claudia said in anguish. 'Rule out this girl, Blaise. She could never be woman enough for you. She's too soft.'

'Is this what it's all about?' Judith asked her brother-in-law quietly. 'Is it *Laura*?'

'I've asked Laura to marry me,' he said sternly. 'Does that answer your question?'

'I guess it does.' Steven answered for himself and his wife. 'And you know what? I'm pleased. In fact, I'm more than pleased. Laura will be peace and serenity in this house.'

'*You* know what you'll be, don't you?' Claudia turned on Laura with devastating swiftness. 'You can see it happening. Blaise desperately wants a son, and when he gets one from you he'll turn his back on you like he did to Virginia. You see, he's a cruel, hard man.'

'And I love him,' Laura watched Claudia's working face with unconcealed pity. 'It's as simple as that. I'm telling you, Claudia, you don't know Blaise at all. He's not cruel. He could never be cruel. Not now or long ago with Virginia.'

Blaise's arms encircled her, drawing her back against the support of his body, but when he spoke, his voice was hard and final. 'Go to bed, Claudia. Go home in the morning and find someone else to love. I've never thought of you in the way you imagined. You can see that now. It's Laura I want, and I've wanted her for a long time.'

'Then tell her about Virginia and Liza,' Claudia hissed at him with what little venomous fire she still had in her. 'Tell her about your sluttish wife. That *illegitimate* kid you call your daughter!'

It was Judith who reached out. With one swift movement she struck her sister across the face with a slap that rang in their ears and turned Claudia into a huddled, crying statue.

'I'm ashamed of you, Claudia,' Judith said in a low, judicious voice. 'Mother and Father would be horrified to hear and see you. I'm so glad the children are asleep and Gran is not here to suffer—*again*. Besides, Laura knows. So you're surprised?' She laughed a little at Claudia's quick reaction. 'Laura is the sort of person one confides in. She's very trustworthy and, moreover, compassionate. It makes no difference to Laura, your story. And why should it? The past is over and I wish Blaise and Laura a bright future. He's got the right woman.'

Claudia drew herself up and incredibly gave a shrug. 'I will never forget you said that, Judith. And now, if you'll all excuse me, I have some packing to do.'

Six weeks later Blaise and Laura were married. Not quietly as they really wanted but to a big social fanfare. People flew into the station from all over the country and many places abroad.

'It's expected, dear,' old Mrs Hunter explained to Laura proudly. 'We Hunters have always been famous for our hospitality and this is a very happy occasion. I couldn't be more grateful to the good Lord for sparing me. Blaise deserves your healing love and I know he is going to make you very, very happy.'

As a prophecy, it was remarkably accurate.

Moving radiantly on Howard's arm, Laura's luminous eyes were fixed on only one person. He stood there with his raven head thrown back, but when she reached him, he turned and looked down at her and his smile was the most revealing she was ever to see in her life. He couldn't look at her so exultantly unless he loved her and desperately needed her for fulfilment.

They faced one another in the garden that was filled with hundreds of guests on plush chairs beneath white-fringed canopies that had been specially erected. No one could possibly have been insensitive to the adoration of the bride, nor the expression on the groom's face as he caught his first sight of her.

Laura was dressed in white, an Edwardian style gown of chiffon and exquisite hand-made lace, a long dress that was ravishing in its perfection and suited her elegant blonde beauty. A filmy leghorn hat, dipping to one side with a cascade of silk roses, shielded her lovely face from the golden rays of the sun. She looked a revelation. The way a girl should look on the wonderful day she became a bride; the innocence and the promise, the reaching for one man's hand, as though there were only one path in life to take and he the man to join her.

Many of the women guests were seen to cry. A lot of them had never realised a man could look at a woman with so much startling passion. The success of the marriage seemed as inevitable as the dawning of the sun on the morrow.

After the ceremony Blaise put his arm around his bride as though he would never let her go and Laura, dazed with happiness, received the warm good wishes of her guests. Paula even threw her arms around her, saying she had never seen a more beautiful bride in her life, and far beyond recalling Paula's incredible treachery, Laura received her stepmother's kiss with a quiet heart.

Jamie was there somewhere with Liza, both children considerably subdued, if only for the moment, with the solemnity of the ceremony and the part they had had to play as Laura's attendants. Of course Laura had Susan and Alison, her special friends, to attend her as well, and they looked flowerlike in their filmy rose and gold dresses, but Laura had frequently been heard to ask one or other of the children to do some important little thing for her. Afterwards she had clasped their suddenly shy little faces in her hands and kissed them with love. She had gifts for them as well—the most beautiful gold locket for Liza and Jamie's first grown-up watch, one he was destined never to part with, though he became a brilliant architect with many fine possessions.

Old Mrs Hunter did not speak at all. She simply gathered Laura to her, then her grandson, and her deepest feelings were communicated to them through the tenderness in her trembling hands. Judith, too, kissed her. Steven, her new brother, both of them pressing her to them, knowing they had found a powerful ally and one who would speak for them. Then there were relatives in plenty, lots of important guests and just plain, ordinary Outback people who had served the Hunter family well in some capacity or other and were relishing this glorious occasion.

The bridal feast was superlative, Jean and Mrs Madden smiling and congratulating one another, determined not to let their few little supremacy battles spoil this most perfect day. Mrs Madden was almost completely over her disability and old Smiler, in the strangest collection of best clothes, had the great good fortune to see the bride. An operation was coming up for Smiler, but he had lived through far worse things in his long life.

The hours slid past in a dream; an iridescent kaleidoscope of spectacle and people. And then it was time to fly out on the first leg of their honeymoon. Not an extended one, because Blaise could not be too long from the station, but with time enough to be wondrously, urgently alone.

They stayed that first night at a very grand hotel, standing at the floor-to-ceiling plate glass windows that encircled their suite and looking out at the brilliantly lit city and the suburbs beyond.

'Feel like dinner?' Blaise murmured, dropping his head so his chin rested on the top of Laura's shining head.

'I think I'm hungry.' She rested back against him, savouring his warmth.

'You didn't eat a thing at the reception.'

'I never eat when I'm excited.'

'Then you must now.'

She turned herself and looked up at him, her eyes like jewels. 'What shall I wear?'

'I don't think we're ever going to top that wedding gown. You looked so beautiful you took everyone's breath away.'

'And you?'

Into his eyes came a swift lick of flame. 'I'm going

to tell you all that. Later.' He bent his head and kissed her lightly, but she could feel the faintest trembling in his lean, powerful body.

In the end he chose for her a very dressy Valentino short evening dress in a vibrant cherry red and they lingered over a superb dinner in the hotel's finest restaurant, which neither of them did justice to, though they did finish the superb Krug they had started out toasting each other with.

Shortly before midnight they instinctively moved together to go back to their suite. Both of them had been deliberately delaying the moment when they would come together; the turbulent maelstrom of sensual pleasure.

Blaise's fingers held Laura's as they walked to their door, electricity in his touch, a shock that left her trembling yet ablaze, as though his body fed flame to hers.

They stopped a few feet from the bed and his fingers closed over her fragile wrist. 'I know what I'll do, I'll undress you.'

'Don't you want any help at all?' She knew it was going to be the most exquisite torture, but she wanted it.

'No.' He smiled at her as he would always smile at her now. The zipper slid down her back and her beautiful taffeta dress sank to the floor. 'Mrs Hunter,' he said.

'My husband.' An incredible tender yearning was filling her.

Other wispy garments pooled to the floor and her breasts were high and tilted as she lifted her arms to him.

'*Laura.*' His voice came against her throat, the merest jagged sigh.

'Darling.'

He covered her open mouth then, engulfing her in sensation so that very soon her limbs turned fluid and he had to support her with his body.

'You're magic!' he muttered.

'*You're* the sorcerer!'

He lifted her then, carrying her to the bed, seeing the deep hunger that was in him matched in her enormous, sparkling eyes.

He took one step away from her, very virile and handsome, the light glossing his bronzed skin, the definite bone structure, and ripped his beautiful jacket off, one lean brown hand going to his Italian silk tie. The tie, incredibly, he had allowed her to buy for him.

'I want you ... I want you ... I *want* you!' she began behind him in a soft, singing chant, watching him move towards her, tall, wide-shouldered, lean-hipped, long-legged, the perfect male body.

'And so, my love,' Blaise murmured thrillingly, 'life begins!'

THE FATHER OF IMPRESSIONISM

Impressionism is a style of painting outdoor subjects, and is characterized by bold strokes of bright color. Seen close up an Impressionist picture with its thick patches of paint makes little sense. But from a short distance the scene falls into place and the painting flickers and vibrates, as if in motion.

Claude Monet, hailed today as the father of Impressionism, was born in 1840 and grew up in the French port city of Le Havre. At nineteen, he settled in Paris to paint, and here began an extended period of hardship.

To save on rent, Monet built a studio-boat from which he painted variations of sunlight and mist on water and riverbank. Friends came to paint with him, Renoir among them, and in 1874 a group of these artists arranged an exhibition in Paris. The response to the group's work ranged from sarcasm to outrage. A critic mockingly called the artists "impressionists," after the title of Monet's painting *Impression: Sunrise*. The artists adopted the label.

Despite extreme poverty and the death of his beloved wife, Monet continued to paint his serene landscapes. By 1880, after almost thirty years of struggle and criticism, Monet finally began to break through to the public. He moved to a country house and settled down to paint willows, water lilies and exotic flowers—often extensive series of single subjects captured at different moments of the day.

In 1923 Monet was nearly blind, yet he continued to paint up to the time of his death in 1926...forever capturing on canvas his poetic impressions of the nature's beauty.

A Harlequin

ROBERTA LEIGH

Collector's Edition

A specially designed collection of six exciting love stories by one of the world's favorite romance writers—Roberta Leigh, author of more than 60 bestselling novels!

1 **Love in Store**	4 **The Savage Aristocrat**
2 **Night of Love**	5 **The Facts of Love**
3 **Flower of the Desert**	6 **Too Young to Love**

Available in August wherever paperback books are sold, or available through Harlequin Reader Service. Simply complete and mail the coupon below.

- -